Alan Sillitoe was born [...] work in various facto[...] control assistant with t[...] 1945.

He enlisted in May 1[...] years on active service i[...] the end of 1949 he was [...] of the service with a hundred per cent disability pension.

He began writing, and lived for six years in France and Spain. His first stories were printed in the *Nottinghamshire Weekly Guardian*. In 1958 *Saturday Night and Sunday Morning* was published, and *The Loneliness of the Long-distance Runner*, which won the Hawthornden Prize for literature, came out the following year. Both these books were made into films.

Further works include *Key to the Door*, *The Ragman's Daughter* and *The General* (both also filmed), *The William Posters Trilogy*, *A Start in Life*, *Raw Material*, *The Widower's Son*, *The Second Chance* – as well as six volumes of poetry. His latest books are *Her Victory*, *The Lost Flying Boat*, *Down from the Hill* and *Life Goes On*. With his wife, Ruth Fainlight, he divides his time between London and a house in Kent.

By the same author

Saturday Night and
  Sunday Morning
The Loneliness of the Long-
  distance Runner
The General
Key to the Door
The Ragman's Daughter
The Death of William
  Posters
A Tree on Fire
A Start in Life
Travels in Nihilon
Raw Materials
Men, Women and Children
The Flame of Life
The Widower's Son
The Storyteller
The Second Chance
Her Victory
The Lost Flying Boat
Down from the Hill
Life Goes On

Poetry
The Rats and Other Poems
A Falling Out of Love and
  Other Poems
Love in the Environs of
  Voronezh
Storm and Other Poems
Snow on the North Side of
  Lucifer
Sun Before Departure
Tides and Stone Walls

Plays
All Citizens Are Soldiers
  (with Ruth Fainlight)
Three Plays

Non-fiction
Road to Volgograd

Essays
Mountains and Caverns

For children
The City Adventures of
  Marmalade Jim
Big John and the Stars
The Incredible Fencing
  Fleas
Marmalade Jim on the
  Farm
Marmalade Jim and the
  Fox

ALAN SILLITOE

Guzman, Go Home

GRAFTON BOOKS
A Division of the Collins Publishing Group

LONDON GLASGOW
TORONTO SYDNEY AUCKLAND

Grafton Books
A Division of the Collins Publishing Group
8 Grafton Street, London W1X 3LA

Published by Grafton Books 1986

First published in Great Britain by
Macmillan and Company Ltd 1968

Copyright © Alan Sillitoe 1968

ISBN 0-586-06566-0

Printed and bound in Great Britain by
Collins, Glasgow

Set in Imprint

All rights reserved. No part of this publication
may be reproduced, stored in a retrieval system,
or transmitted, in any form, or by any means,
electronic, mechanical, photocopying, recording or
otherwise, without the prior permission of
the publishers.

This book is sold subject to the condition that
it shall not, by way of trade or otherwise, be
lent, re-sold, hired out or otherwise circulated
without the publisher's prior consent in any
form of binding or cover other than that
in which it is published and without a similar
condition including this condition being
imposed on the subsequent purchaser.

CONTENTS

REVENGE	7
CHICKEN	34
CANALS	40
THE ROAD	66
THE ROPE TRICK	81
ISAAC STARBUCK	107
GUZMAN, GO HOME	142

REVENGE

The service was over, and we signed the book, stood outside the late-English Perpendicular nondescript church, while the buffed-up blackened eye of the camera fixed us forever in the bewildered yet happy world.

Confetti snowed down, coloured snow, tips of spring flowers falling over our bent backs as we got into the car. Life was beginning, and we laughed, never wondering whether or not we would cry at the far end of it all. The preacher's claptrap still fed my humour, though it wasn't long before I began to look back on it as one big farce. My mates didn't even grin when I agreed to a church wedding. They thought I was quite right to give in to her, the spineless lot, and so I was glad to change into another department where the hypocrisy of friendship hadn't had time to jell, so that we could all concur how soft I'd been to slide back on my principles, even though it hurt me to say so.

I was nearing forty, and Caroline who became my wife had just turned thirty, so it was late for both of us. But every old sock finds an old shoe, as those at work laughingly put it. With my parents dead, I lived alone in the house I had just finished buying, and that as an only son I had grown up in. It was a house of the better sort, with three floors instead of two, and set a few yards back from the pavement. My bride now came there for the reception.

She looked so beautiful, among all our friends at the table, that I wondered how she'd come to marry me, which explains why I'd let us be spliced in church perhaps. But looks never counted for much between us. I'm well set up and stocky, with all my hair still and swept back neat. What's more I've never been got at by illness. All that bothered me was a tapeworm in Gibraltar during the war, but it wasn't so rare as to be a real sickness, though such a thing growing inside me, no matter how much they pulled it out, took weeks to get rid of. In fact I became so badly that I was shipped home, and sometimes I wonder if I'm not still harbouring it, I feel so jumpy. Maybe it's just the memory, and time will tell, though it has enough to live on in the meantime if it really is down there chewing away.

I was looking at the darling I'd married, tall and thin-faced, with fine fair hair that I hoped she'd now grow long (though she never did), and good features when she was pleasantly smiling. Otherwise I'd stick my thumb towards the earth and enjoy feeling a swine – but it's too early to start being hard on myself. I'd only met her six months before, and what all the hurry was I couldn't now say. Certainly, I didn't know then that she'd gone through a bout of mental trouble at twenty. Even if I had known there'd have been no backing out, but rather I would have worn the fact in my buttonhole to show everyone what a noble sort I was.

So many presents piled on the sideboard gave me a funny feeling, a disturbance I couldn't remark on because it hardly existed, and in any case it wouldn't have been polite to do so at such a time. Around the glory of the cake was a spread-out zone of toasters, dinner-services and tea-sets, electric blankets, transistor radios, horseshoes and telegrams, records and ashtrays, plastic fruit and paper flowers, kettles and bedside lights, that everyone looked avidly over, stuff which almost brought tears into Caroline's eyes when she passed them by to take off her dress upstairs.

Two rooms had been opened into one, and the space was full, tables put together down the middle and bordered by every chair in the house, plus a few brought by her brother in his brand-new estate car. Trimmings were up, lights on, and drink was flowing. What could go wrong with such a spread of cake and salad, ham and wine? I said so in my speech after we'd all set to. A friend from work mumbled something about going at it like a bull at a gate, but I stopped him in mid-flight. I didn't like a thing like that, because I considered it the vilest kind of talk. Times were changing, and there was no call for smutty humour any more. It brought silence for a few moments, but I noticed how Caroline smiled her thanks, and that was good enough for me. As for Bernie, I'd plaster him when I got back to work, unless it slipped my mind, which it most likely would. I was glad again. The lights were back on in the attics of my brain – except when they glimpsed that sideboard-pile of presents.

'Ladies and gentlemen!' I shouted, and they fell quiet. 'Friends, boys and girls, I've come here today' – they were already rocking with laughter because it was good clean fun, and I was known as a bit of a jokester – 'to let you know that I am now . . . oh my God! I've forgotten the word. Now, what was the word I wanted? Eh? Tell me somebody, please.'

'Married!' Bernie shouted, my old friend.

'Married. Thank you. That was it. To tell you that I am now *married*! You can't know how much it means to me when I tell you that, but I thought I'd explain the presence of all this food and drink, and those gifts you can see behind me, all that fantastic stack of gifts . . . otherwise you might wonder!'

'Good old Richard.'

'Get on with it then!' That was from Bernie again. He never could leave well alone.

'So here's a toast to my presence here, and to Caroline, and to all of you who've come to honour us. We left it rather late, but better that, I feel, than the other way. I'm not much of a hand at weddings, this being my first. I didn't go to my parents', like some people I've met who might have done, so excuse any lack of formality, dear friends.' I was sweating now, and more and more toasts didn't help. Neither did the food, which I wasn't able to touch. The arrangement was that we'd stay in the house that night, and leave for Hastings at ten the next morning, and train times kept going round in my head.

The only thing now was to render a couple of songs for them, which I did. My voice was good, and I'd often entertained at friends' houses and on bus-outings from work. I gave them, but mainly for Caroline's sake, because I knew she loved both: 'I'll Walk Beside You' and 'Abide With Me'. But that was the last time I did any such thing, which was a pity, because I was always proud of my voice.

One by one they left, wishing me luck and happiness. I felt like going with them, shaking hands with the bride and invisible bridegroom, bestowing on them the best of health, then vanishing into the autumn dusk of chip smells, fog and freedom. Yet it was my wedding, proved by those glittering and intimidating presents on the sideboard, above all by that pagoda of pots, the kingpin dinner-service in dazzling flowers and cottages. I couldn't believe I'd have to use them for the rest of my life, drink out of them, eat off them, warm myself by them. One or two people didn't want to leave, or were too drunk to do so, and the trouble is I wasn't too drunk to envy them. But I remembered my position as man and husband of the house, and helped them out into the street.

Everything had gone like clockwork and by the book. The last women to depart had washed the pots and straightened up. Neatness made the house so barren, yet I'd been looking forward to this moment for weeks and, I believe, so had Caroline. The fire was burning well, and now we could sit by it and relax, laugh over the day's routine.

I kicked off with a harmless enough remark: 'It went easier than I expected.'

'Perfect,' she smiled, 'thanks to you, Richard. The service was beautiful. "Whom God hath joined together let no man put asunder".'

'Ay,' I assented. 'They know how to say it.'

'That was it, wasn't it?'

'It was.' I was conscious and absolutely clear in my brain of the effect every word was going to have before I said it, though it had no brake whatsoever on my self-control. 'They ought to get out an EP record of the marriage service.'

'What a marvellous idea.'

'Add on the first night and make it an LP.'

'What, Richard?'

'The morning after would make it an album, I expect. Sell like hot cakes.'

'Are you a bit jangled?' she asked, having just caught the reek that all wasn't well.

'If you like.'

'Can I get you some aspirin?' My head was burning, but I said no, that I was all right. She smiled, forgiving when there was no need to be. If there had been, the balloon would have gone up already. 'You don't have any regrets, do you love?'

It was too early to say. Did she think that nothing more was to come? 'None,' I said, putting my arms around her. I loved her even more than I loved myself, and no man could say fairer than that. I was taken out of myself, as happy as if I were flying over a desert that was just sprouting flowers again. My arms tightened, and her head leaned comfortably on my shoulder. I'd drunk enough that day and perhaps it helped, yet it was something more that set my blood melting. Certainly I didn't have to tell myself that I was four hours married in order to feel all the breeding and manners ever instilled into me drifting away.

She stood up quickly. 'I can't, Richard. It must be in the right way. Not yet.'

'Why not?' I shouldn't have said that, but it came before I could help myself, throwing me back on to a filthy pavement at the butt-end of summer – which is about the only sort of earth I've ever known in my deeper moments.

'It was the same before we were married,' she cried. 'Always in too much of a hurry. It's almost uncouth.'

The 'almost' clawed right through me, a mincing qualification that would have made a plain 'uncouth' laughable by comparison. It bit deep, sounded like the worst of insults, because a real insult is when somebody tells something about yourself you've half-known all along. That's the cut. If you are told something you couldn't possibly have known, you just laugh, because it's not true, what you could not know.

I was unable to answer, and she thought I was sulking in order to get my own back. 'Why spoil it?' she said. 'Would you like a glass of sherry?'

I screwed out a smile. Maybe Bernie had been right after all about a bull at a gate. 'Please, love.'

'A slice of ham?' she called from the kitchen.

Blood in my mouth: I'd bitten my tongue. 'No thanks.' I looked around and the spread of presents shrivelled my brain. It was a carnival that lacked a death's head, skull and crossbones and the King Snapdragon of the lot. I closed my eyes, then opened them with the thought that if I didn't they might stay shut forever. I spied a heavy poker standing by the fire, one of the gifts already unpacked, squared-off at one end and falling to a point, a beautiful instrument made by a couple of friends at work, the firm's metal but their skill and sweat – and regard for me.

I picked it up, weighed and balanced it, lifted it high and stood over the whole patchwork regalia. I've always taken pride in my arm strength, felt it gathering now in my shoulders for a job to be bloody well done.

There was a shout from the doorway: 'Richard!'

Her face was white, thinner than I'd ever seen it, and I saw then how much this so-called marriage ceremony had worn her out. I was filled with pity, which I knew to be good and honest because I lowered the poker.

'What are you doing?' she righteously demanded.

'Feeling the weight of it. It's a lovely piece of work. Last forever, if you ask me.'

She put the tray down. 'You were going to do something you'd never forgive yourself for. And I wouldn't want you to do that, because I've got to live with you.' She was always lucid during trouble, and I admired her for it. We looked at each other. She couldn't stand the silence like I could, after such a day, and I can't blame her. 'Oh dear,' she said in sudden exultation as if that organ music was starting all over again. 'I was right.'

I had a blinding vision of our four wounded parents squatting among that trash like a collection of grinning gnome-faced jugs, prophesying and winking at each other over the idiotic unknown step I'd taken with the darling of my life, their hats askew and atremble in delight at what we were about to do to ourselves, which was all that they had done, right to the point of outliving regret and bitterness by the time old age came upon them, which lasted a few years and enabled them to fix a grin forever that advised us to live through the rottenness like them, because we'd come to enjoy it in the end and join them in helping to pass it down to oncoming innocents forever.

The force of my arm drove a canyon down that dinner-service and split it asunder, quartered and shattered it by wave after wave of strength and agony. It was rocking, knocking every transistor out of its pocket, buckling ashtrays, irons, pot-dogs, bowls, bows, a shop-window of all the catalogue-goods of servitude spending under my poker quicker than they'd ever reach the dustbin by normal wear and tear. When I thought there was nothing left, I noticed a walnut polished biscuit-barrel untouched at one corner on the edge of the bomb damage. Coaxing it into the middle – no cooper would ever own it from henceforth – I splayed it flat like a star.

I must have taken my time over it, because Caroline had her coat on, a suitcase by her side that she'd gone to Butlin's with the year before. 'Right,' I said, sitting exhausted on one of the stools, 'going home, are you?'

'Yes,' she answered coolly, while my own breath could hardly move.

'But this is your home, so let's have your coat off. Put that case away and be sensible.'

'You really want me to?'

'Yes.'

She waited a while, the silence on her side now. 'All right, Richard, I will stay.'

I didn't like the way she looked at me while taking off her coat, but then, had I any right to?

Every time Caroline came up in the morning and placed a cup of tea at my bedside she said: 'How do you know it's not poisoned?' and walked downstairs again, leaving me to wonder.

I knew it wasn't, but how could a man be sure? Not me, certainly, because even in the face of anyone as good as gold I'd never have the nerve to be sure of them. Blind love and adoration would only make me suspicious, while the pure hatred I was now getting couldn't make it much worse. But the world had to go on, and I never knew whether or not my tea was poisoned till I'd stepped on the bus for work, for if the gripes hadn't struck by then I could begin to hope again. Usually the bus was so cold I even stopped sweating. It was a bad winter.

According to a newspaper read at lunchbreak one day, marital difficulties are the greatest cause of divorce. As if I didn't know, being a realistic man. I've known some people though, and I won't mention any names, who seem to regard marriage as a pact wherein each party promises to drive the other mad or kill in the attempt. But it appears to me that most divorces come about because people grow bored with each other – though Caroline and I never got bored, and consequently we had to find another way to split up.

For Christmas she gave me a box of Cuban cigars, plastered with labels looking like birth-certificates and hundred-pound notes. She sat with a loving smile, anticipating thanks, while I spent five minutes with a penknife trying to find the slit of the lid, getting more impatient till I broke the box from end to end along the wrong side, cracked it to splinters so that wood and cigars and bits of label tumbled on to the rug. 'I'm just not good at opening boxes of cigars,' I said.

She stood up and walked out of the room, vowing never to speak to me again, but later that night when I was taking off my shirt she said: 'Hasn't anyone ever told you that patience and understanding are needed in this world?' She spoke with lips close together, as if to stop her false teeth falling out should she grow too emotional – but she had no false teeth.

'Not yet, they haven't,' I answered with a smile.

'What you want,' she said sharply, 'is for some barbarian to come along and civilize you.'

I fell in love with her again, kept falling in love at forty as much as I had done at twenty. When I admitted this she called me a case of arrested development, not to have altered in all those years. The fact that I'd married someone like her, she said, proved it.

The trouble was, I'd married late, for while living was pleasant I took my time and held it off. When the world was good I felt no reason to be good back to it. I worked too hard for that. I know now that I'd been selfish, but if I saw in those days all that I know now I don't see how I could have gone on living, so it's a good job I didn't. You're too busy making what's in store for you to think about the future when it comes – or when it doesn't, I told myself. The world's got to go round, after all.

She called me a monster of selfishness when I told her all this, and maybe I did become one, yet I wasn't too selfish not to fall in with her wish and have a church wedding. I've never believed in religious claptrap, but I loved her, and she was fervent in wishing for it, to say the least, and love makes a man honourable in that he'll do anything for his beloved. He might undo it all again later, though I wasn't to know that at the time.

Love is like childhood – golden to recall. Galling moments are forgotten, and all those wasted words and waves of anguish vanish before the mystic flights of going to bed, fall like lees of sand to the sea-bottom. I know it, especially if I keep telling myself, over and over again. But I can place the end of what might be called our love with the exactitude of a carpenter's rule.

We were lying on the bed one summer's evening after making love, naked and calm, and full of affection, even though our modesty had gone. Her face looked at mine, and she smiled, beautiful and tender, as if we had never known anyone else but each other and had been continually in a state of sublime love from the very first moment. Our kisses were pure, the prime height of emotional life. Caroline smiled again, and as I looked at her an unexpected voice, out of place but unmistakable, came into my mind and said to her: 'Goodbye, goodbye, goodbye.' She was not allowed to hear it, and I smiled back, alarmed yet thrilled at the intruding voice, which I knew to be as true as the dead wood in my heart.

But it wasn't over yet – not by a long way. We had our distractions, being a serious couple. She read magazines and romantic fiction, while I went in for a better class of book because I was hard to satisfy in that spiritual way. Otherwise I might have gone to church on Sunday morning like she kept on doing. But I'd only twiddle my thumbs there, want to take a book out and read till it was all over. So I didn't shame her by going, preferred to brood and read, and hug my mood in the hope of becoming familiar with what was happening inside myself. I'd never allow any preacher to tell me anything, or stop me knowing myself. I sometimes thought I might like to, but the fact was that I couldn't. I never talked much to other men, being a foreman at work, which gave me some advantage in that at least I could talk to myself with some possibility of not being misunderstood.

In spite of our ups and downs, and the times when we knew in our hearts that it was finished for sure, we were in love for a long time – two years to be precise and show you the exact nature of our optimism. We'd occasionally talk about what we'd do if we had all the money in the world, the charities she'd help, the places I'd visit, the common joy of having no set work. What I omitted in my cowardly way to remind her was that if I hadn't been going to work forty hours a week we wouldn't have lasted together three months, because our bitterest quarrels usually took place when she got back from evensong on Sunday night. She walked in in her lilac-blue hat and high-heeled shoes, pale suit, umbrella if it was raining, and at that night's supper when I'd been longest away from my workshop of friends and machines our fatal, final, common incompatibilities would break in on us like vixens.

One Saturday morning, when we were clearing away breakfast things, she looked straight and tenderly into my eyes. 'Richard, I love you. You know that, don't you?'

We stood by the kitchen door: 'Yes, I know you do' – and kissed her.

'I'd never do anything to hurt you, you know that. You're the only man I've ever loved, in spite of everything.'

'Sweetheart,' I said, wondering a little bit what was up, but thinking she was just being affectionate.

The vicar came to see her that afternoon. I'd normally have been at a football match, but the pitch was deep in snow, so I sat in the living room playing one of my classical records – I forget which. I had to turn the stereo off when he came in – though two frustrations in one day didn't seem overmuch for me at the time.

I hadn't seen him since that day in his cold and draughty church. Not that I had any real dislike for him, for no doubt it would have been somebody else who married us, even if only in a registry office. He was a good man as far as I knew, with a harassed wife and four kids, who lived in a crumbling vicarage opposite his place of work. An ex-RAF man (like myself, who'd been an airframe fitter through the war), he was about fifty, bald, well built, and might have been a stoker in another age.

Caroline gave an embarrassed hello, then went away busily to get tea ready. The parson sat opposite me by the fire, a sweat on his face in spite of the snow, which I suppose he'd hurried through in order to get out of.

'Some people like snow,' he grinned, 'because they find it picturesque, but I think it's a damned nuisance, really.'

'I have inside work myself,' I said, wanting to be agreeable. 'As long as it doesn't hold up the buses, and I'm able to get there. "Whom God hath joined let no man put asunder" – especially concerning his work.' I suddenly had an idea as to why he'd come to see us, and in a detached sort of way could feel my heart choking on its own blood because of it. It was no good. I didn't love Caroline any more. If one can ever believe in God one can only do so when one is in love. To believe at such a time is the most sublime state of all, I am sure, but I had lost even love, and therefore everything. He had come a bit too late for me to credit his help, though at the same time he could never have been early enough, either.

'To a certain extent you're right,' he argued, 'but man was created before work.'

'I always thought God put in a good six days,' I answered, 'before he clocked off for the weekend and sat down to rest.'

'All right, Mr Butler, but you know, Caroline is very unhappy about the way your marriage is going, and as she is a good member of our parish church, and as I had the great pleasure of marrying you both, I simply think that it must then be my duty as a friend and a Christian to ask if I can help you in your trouble. You must excuse this unannounced visit to your home but I imagine, rightly,' – here he gave a fair laugh – 'that you might not have stayed in if I'd given you notice. And I couldn't talk to you at church because you don't come, I'm sorry to say.'

'Was this Caroline's idea?'

'Well, yes. In a way it was. But I can't say exactly.'

I stood up. 'Mind your own business, and clear out.'

Caroline was at the door, our best wedding-present tea-tray loaded: 'Richard, what are you saying? Please!' She put the tray down to unload it, as if such activity would diminish the saltpetre air of the room.

'I'll solve my own problems,' I cried at them both.

'We were made to help our fellow-men,' the parson said in a quiet and dignified way. He stood and took me by the elbow, surprised at my violence, though confident he could handle it. But his self-assurance, sparking from insolent generations of bossiness, drew blood from my eyeballs. I was surprised at still being able to talk.

'But not to preach to them,' I shouted. 'What gives

you a right to try to understand me?' I snapped his hand away. 'You've been to college? You've got faith? That'll never be enough, mate. If I need help – and I'm not so sure it's me that needs it – then it'll come from inside me in its own good time. You'll just mix it up and push it back. So get out and find some slobbering grateful arthritic terrified godfearing parishioner who's ready to peg out and needs your ministrations. Then get the Good Lord on the blower and tell Him how good you've been. Reverse the charges if you can't afford it. Go on, get out of my house.'

He didn't even say goodbye, and picked up his coat to get it on in the snow. I stood on my own two feet, though aching to hug the earth in my black piercing rage. Pride had got me like a rat, and wouldn't let go. I was left with Caroline, whose big eyes shone mistily from a pale face. Where had I seen it before? Greens and yellows and long hair, large eyes like candleflames, pupils reaching up to the flaring tip, face derelict and phosphorous, all of it looking at bestial barbaric me through a heavy glass window. But the glass broke, and I staggered across the room at a savage blow from the tray.

I didn't go to work for three days. Nor did I eat during that time, and I think it was this more than me actually hitting her back which finally made her turn the way she did. If I'd just hit her and carried on as if nothing had happened, things might in some strange way have got better between us, in spite of my inability at the moment to see how they ever could. But in breaking the normal routine of life I had cracked, and this disconcerted her so much that she could never forgive me.

I went in the spare room and lay on the single bed without a mattress, would not open the door in spite of her sobbing and knocking. In my darkness I railed at her having called in a parson to try and sort out our troubles (which after all were only a way of life and could have been stuck to the end of our days) so that the more I brooded on it the smaller my heart became. I'd grown up proud and hardworking and independent, lived by all those dead-true clichés that only mean so much when somebody spits on them.

If I belched on my way to work I'd know I hadn't been poisoned. The sun promised and sweet April threatened, a fusing scene of unease and well-being which made the streets feel friendlier and more protective than on other days. Mist was blue and fresh in early morning, the first breath of skinless springtime over the city, and if I didn't inhale too deeply on the doorstep it smelled pleasantly nostalgic and reminded me of the happiness I'd once had. Fortunately it didn't pierce deeply enough to get through to the irrevocable layer of smoke and swamp underneath, which would make me wish I hadn't lit that cigarette after putting on my hat, and that I had never got married in the first place. The trees were less brittle and blue on this particular day, faintly streaked with the emerald of spreading buds. It was a more colourful morning than I could ever remember, and it didn't occur to me to wonder why until I reached for the rail of the bus and slid back into the gutter.

Since my encounter with the parson she'd been out to get me. 'How do you know it isn't poisoned?' she'd smile on bringing my tea up in the morning, said it so often that after a couple of months I didn't believe it was any more. If I'd had any sense I should have booted her out the first time she said it, but it had always been my biggest fault, to think quick and act slow.

I might have known something was wrong when she said goodbye in an almost affectionate tone. The tea tasted strange, but she said the milk had gone off, and I thought no more about it till my legs weakened and my heart raced, and it burst as I reached out for the bus. She'd been grinding up sleeping pills, and because of overtime I hadn't got in till ten the night before. I fell into bed and slept like an ox, and welcomed the bedside tea next morning with a smile.

I woke up in hospital, and for the first time in my life I both thought and acted quick at the same time. What made me spout the right words I don't know, but it wasn't reason, and it wasn't emotion either. Nor was it a sense of love and protection I owed to my wife, because from then on Caroline would never be a wife to me again. We'd mean nothing to each other. She had brought on us the law of the jungle by trying to kill me, and I'd never let myself live in a jungle. And yet, who knows really what the jungle is like, and what goes on in the mind of animals who live in it? Do animals kill more of one another than men do? Maybe this was spinning in my mind when I woke up and blurted out: 'I didn't mean to kill myself. I took the tablets by mistake.' I smiled when I saw how easy it was to make them believe me no matter what Caroline might say.

But she knew how to handle her side of life too; came to see me during my few days in hospital, walked up to the bed with a bunch of flowers and a widow's smile, as if just back from my burial service at church. We'd finished each other off with such utter completeness that it almost made me sad. I wanted to shout to the nurse: 'Take her out! Go on, or I'll really kill myself!' – except that it would have showed up my lie on coming out of the dark.

She sat by the bed, so triumphant I could almost

have fallen in love with her for the last time.

'What did you tell them?' she asked.

'That I didn't mean to kill myself. What nice flowers.'

'They're for you.'

'They'd have looked more fitting on my grave. Take them away.'

'I'll ask one of the nurses to put them in water as I go out. Why did you tell them that?' She straightened my pillow, all wifelike.

'Will you do it again?'

Her smile was wide, right at the deep end. 'Do what?'

'Try to murder me.'

A blush of anger went over her. 'I don't know what you're talking about.'

I laughed, really happy for the first time that she hadn't succeeded. 'That's the stuff. Better to have it on your conscience than me on mine.' The nurse, smiling a young beautiful unencumbered smile, came up with my tea-tray.

'You always were good at self-sacrifice,' Caroline said.

'Better than sacrifice,' I quipped. 'Don't go. Let them see how you love me, or they'll suspect you tried to kill me. Stay and pour my tea.'

Tears were in her eyes, and she stood up. 'How can you joke about it?'

'Look,' I pleaded, 'let's go hand-in-hand into the loony-bin: they'll separate us at the gate, but what an end for us! What a gesture! You can show me the way there since you've been in already.'

'I hope it's not true,' she said, 'that men and women aren't made to live together.'

'I know two that aren't, anyway.'

'You are mad,' she said. 'Now I do know.'

'Get away,' I cried. 'Don't come here to torment me. I forgive you, so what more do you want?' And I did forgive her, because that was the only thing left for me to free myself from her completely.

It was the end, and should have been the beginning, but I stamped it right out of us. Some people split up after ten years in a state of emotional squalor, a decade of under-development, but at least we'd done better than that, in about half the time. Our marriage had been a terrifying mistake which had been allowed to go on only through inanition and neurosis. I for one couldn't go back. I didn't want to. And there were certain things I wouldn't go forward to, either. What have I got to lose? I wondered. Everything, I told myself, but lose it, nevertheless, because underneath the love you have for someone else, the battle for your own survival goes on even more remorselessly.

It was the end, also, of what went into the psychiatrist's tape-recorder. They wanted to hear about my childhood and the earliest memories of family life, but I was only willing to tell them what had been bothering me. I've reconstructed the tape out of my head, because I naturally never got a copy of it. I spent a long time in that office, sitting in an ordinary leather armchair, and talking while those infernal wheels of the tape-machine slowly resolved.

When I first went in the two psychiatrists were chatting normally about what was on at the pictures and what books they'd been reading, altogether ignoring me for a few minutes, as if this was part of their policy. Then I was offered a cigarette, which I was glad of, though they never really put me at ease. Doctor Brown, the one in charge, was short, slim, and had ginger hair, and reminded me of a man who works at the factory – under me. Yet I was half-afraid of them, tardy at going in and diffident when I got there, taking the lift to their big room of an office in a building behind the council house.

Since I'd admitted trying to kill myself the idea of my going there was rather insisted on, though at least I was able to choose a good private man recommended by my own GP. I didn't want my brain chopping about just because I'd reacted with the finer instinct of an animal in trying not to get the same thing done or worse to Caroline. It was bad enough having the neighbours point at me when I walked up the street, bad for any man to stand, while she was talked to with deference and understanding because she had a husband who was sick in the head. Once your pride starts to go, the wind takes it a long way. Still, she needed people to talk to her more than I needed them to talk to me. I never spoke another word to her, because, when I'd said it was the end between us, that was the way I made it turn out. I've always been a moral man who realizes his value to society, but there's a limit to what one can be expected to take – or should be. Social laws are to be kept up to a point because they make life easier among the pain and squalor, but when you stray by mistake into a swamp you are obliged to fight for your life and get out of it. If you can't keep your dignity, then all laws have to be thrown overboard.

During that long talk to the psychiatrist I held on to mine, though it wasn't easy, doing something no part of my soul wanted to, yet having to whether I liked it or not. I simply told my story, and almost felt pleased that they and the tape were listening to me, sensed the good that might come if I gave myself into it, the comfort at being able to spout hour after hour about myself and my so-called troubles and having no one to help me back, only to help me when and if they could. I suppose that was the nearest I got to real madness, because there was nothing wrong with me, seeing how they should have had someone else under the arc-lights.

'Doctor Ridgeway and I will go through this tape,' Brown said, 'and we'll have another session at the same time next week. All we need do in your case is continue these little talks for a while.'

He seemed lighthearted about it, and I can't blame him, since he was dealing with a sane man. Maybe other people he treats are sane also. Still, I was thankful it wasn't as unpleasant as I'd imagined, and that I didn't have reason to wish that Caroline hadn't underestimated the dose necessary to kill me.

The drizzle and mist of the city felt good outside, mid-morning traffic quietened by it. A comforting sense of freedom fell on me as I stood in the doorway and lit a cigarette before stepping into it. I'd go for a cup of coffee before taking the bus home. Yet the gulf seemed to be actually and physically under my feet, and I tried to step lightly in my walk. It was now, having talked it out, that I felt as if there was nothing left between me and Caroline, and in another way between me and the world. We were finished, pulling ourselves apart and to pieces, and I thought for a minute that every man and woman married or living together were really also in this state, the whole of their way of life about to fly apart. And you might ask, what would we have then? Well, you tell me.

But I was fed up with the past, after all that tapework. To think so much about the past is like a desperate and unhappy person running back to his mother for comfort. Life would be so much easier if what you thought and what you did bore some relationship to each other. And yet when I felt for the macintosh on my arm, and realized that I'd left it in the psychiatrist's office, I had a clean and uncomfortable feeling that they did in too many vital ways.

I went up on the lift, and back in again. There was no receptionist to announce me, but I didn't think it mattered, since they were such pleasant informal people. Those inside didn't notice my entrance, being so involved in what they were listening to. An inane tune was jigging through my head, and this may have helped me to remain self-absorbed and unnoticed for so long.

Hearing them replay the tape, it was now that I properly enumerated the furnishings of the office. Desk, pictures, books, three chairs – how bare and empty it was, how hollow now that I stood in as one of them, but for a minute unbeknown to them, no longer part of the furniture, listening to my own voice going towards every corner of the room. I'd heard myself on tape before, so recognized its low-keyed, precise, cocksure, rambling vibration touching off their laughter.

Doctor Brown, who was controlling the machine, switched it to another section of my talk that he was anxious for them to hear. All three were in on it, one a tall broad man, as well as those I already knew. 'He tried to kill himself, and now he says it was his wife who tried to murder him.'

'Delusions of paranoia,' said the new man knowingly.

'Listen to this then,' laughed Doctor Brown, and clicked the reel forward with as much zeal as if the forthcoming funny bit had actually been made up by him, and he wanted the credit for it, so that they could gag about it all through lunch.

So on my voice went, telling of my fight with the parson. At first I couldn't believe they were amused by me, and my mind was flitting around inside itself searching for some parallel motive which might be entertaining them. It was as if, while listening seriously to my talk, they remembered a joke spent between them an hour before and were merely laughing at that. But they were too engrossed in the tape for such to be true, which was also lucky, in that I stayed by the door some time before anyone noticed me. The pain was compounded when part of me also, on hearing their continual laughter, thought that my long confession was funny, and I felt grateful to them for laughing at it, and almost wanted to join in and relax about it with them. But this was only a passing slim impulse – which was the forerunner of the most total black rage I've ever felt. It was beyond shame, spoiled vanity, insult, not even a matter of them being wrong in what they were doing. Everything in my mind was quick and clear, and I've never known black anger to do that, because it left my judgement free when it seemed more necessary than ever in my life before or since.

They flicked the reel, and it hummed along till it settled on the final meeting with my wife by the hospital bedside. They even found this hilarious, but to me it was interesting, my carefully rehearsed story that had been going through my head for weeks at last pinned down. I didn't think it funny though, and wanted them to stop joking about it so that I could follow what was being said, as if it weren't me on the tape at all.

'*You always were good at self-sacrifice,*' Caroline said.

'*Better than sacrifice,*' I quipped. '*Don't go. Let them see how you love me, or they'll suspect you tried to kill me. Stay and pour my tea.*'

Tears were in her eyes, and she stood up. '*How can you joke about it?*'

'Look,' I pleaded, 'let's go hand-in-hand into the loony-bin: they'll separate us at the gate, but what an end for us! What a gesture! You can show me the way there since you've been in already.'

'I hope it's not true,' she said, 'that men and women aren't made to live together.'

'I know two that aren't, anyway.'

'You are mad,' she said. 'Now I do know.'

'Get away,' I cried. 'Don't come here to torment me. I forgive you, so what more do you want?' And I did forgive her, because that was the only thing left for me to free myself from her completely.

They laughed. 'Priceless,' said Doctor Brown.

'Turn it to the wedding, then,' said his colleague.

'Let's have lunch first. We'll go right through it this afternoon.' Nevertheless he flicked back the tape to the marriage part, as if it were going to play them out like a signature tune. 'The thing is,' he said, 'these damn schizos give me the horrors. Which is why I listen to them, I suppose.'

'Must be,' said the other, with a dry laugh.

Then Doctor Brown saw me.

I'd been listening to the tape, true, but also I spied a heavy walking-stick standing in a corner. My rage was back in full, and so was my clarity, and they gave me wolfish strength. The swing of it made a magic circle around me. I wasn't the one at bay, because I heard their voices asking me to put it down, almost pleading. 'It wasn't nice, ethical, or clever,' I said, 'to laugh at me.'

Down came a blow that shot the tape out and up into the air, sent it spiralling towards the ceiling as if the flies up there were holding a victory parade. What was left in the other half also ticker-taped up, coils of brown ribbon shooting and snapping over the room, and all three afraid to touch me or move in case I turned on them, which in my finely conscious state I had no intention of doing, though they were too cowardly to realize it.

'I trusted you,' I shouted, with another burst at the disintegrating tape jerking and squirting away from me as I finally threw down the walking-stick and went out of the room.

I worked on a building-site in London as a labourer, a very high building, and all the men wondered why I had so much nerve, how it was possible that after so short a time on the job I wasn't in the least afraid of such terrifying heights. The foreman had a good word for me, told me I knew what to do without much explanation and carried out my work calmly. He talked about giving me my own gang on a big job coming up the following year.

As I worked, so high up, there was the sound of aeroplanes passing all day towards the airport, gracefully sloping down between me and the sky, beautiful pieces of machinery that are so much more perfect than men, and more useful. The sight of them inspired me one minute and depressed me the next. If it weren't for the fact that men had made them, I would no longer have wanted to go on living. I was often sad at night when I could no longer see those beautiful machines. Yet I could still hear them as I lay trying to sleep, thinking that aeroplanes had replaced the old romantic noise of trains and train-whistles, and that one could fly a much longer way in them.

Back on earth my escape had been made, out of the swamp I'd landed in but couldn't swim in because there were too many monsters out for my arms and legs. I thought at first I might be brought back for what I did in the psychiatrists' office and for not carrying on my treatment with them. But I heard nothing, touch wood. Perhaps they realized what damage they'd done, and so made it all right for me. If so, it's the least (and most) they could do, and those particular ones are the sort of people a human being can deal with, if he ceases at a lucky and crucial moment to be a human being who is dependent on them – which is the least I can say for such wayward immoral bastards.

I work hard on my job, because at the moment not much else is left, though it will be. Often on my fetching and carrying high above the river I look up into the sky. Clouds are shrouds to wrap the sun in, hustle it away to doom and ruin. But I can look down as well. In my house there are many mansions – with different coloured wallpaper, maybe, and it's a hard house to get out of, especially if you are walking on the roof, and you can look between your feet into every room at once.

I was looking down at the crowds beckoning me back to earth, but, damn them, I would not go till I was ready, not without the safe wings of flying which I felt growing in place of my arms. I would not live among them any more, not in such impersonal chaos. When I go down I might finally end up in the place I'd tried to avoid all my life, though it was true that Caroline has already been there before me without ever actually having said what it was like. I thought that if I went there she would sooner or later join me, and I didn't want that. I imagined it to be a pretty ordered sort of existence, too much so, as I mildly walked towards the edge of the girder and began to climb down for dinner-break.

Life is long, long enough always to start again. The

black pitch of energy is inexhaustible in the barrel, the spirit-fire burning underneath to keep it always at the boil and bubble. Nothing can stop it, not in me. And if we ever meet again, maybe we'll meet as equals.

CHICKEN

ONE Sunday Dave went to visit a workmate from his foundry who lived in the country near Keyworth. On the way back he pulled up by the laneside to light a fag, wanting some warmth under the leaden and freezing sky. A hen strutted from a gap in the hedge, as proud and unconcerned as if it owned the land for miles around. Dave picked it up without getting off his bike and stuffed it in a sack-like shopping-bag already weighted by a stone of potatoes. He rode off, wobbling slightly, not even time to kill it, preferring in fact the boasting smiles of getting it home alive, in spite of its thumps and noise.

It was nearly teatime. He left his bike by the back door, and walked through the scullery into the kitchen with his struggling sack held high in sudden light. His mother laughed: 'What have you done, picked up somebody's best cat?'

He took off his clips. 'It's a live chicken.'

'Where the hell did you get that?' She was already suspicious.

'Bought it in Keyworth. A couple of quid. All meat, after you slit its gizzard and peel off the feathers. Make you a nice pillow, mam.'

'It's probably got fleas,' Bert said.

He took it from the sack, held it by both legs with one hand while he swallowed a cup of tea with the other. It was a fine plump bird, a White Leghorn hen feathered from tail to topnotch. Its eyes were hooded, covered, and it clucked as if about to lay eggs.

'Well,' she said, 'we'll have it for dinner sometime next week' – and told him to kill it in the backyard so that there'd be no mess in her clean scullery, but really because she couldn't bear to see it slaughtered. Bert and Colin followed him out to see what sort of a job he'd make of it.

He set his cap on the window-sill. 'Get me a sharp knife, will you, somebody?'

'Can you manage?' Colin asked.

'Who are you talking to? Listen, I did it every day when I was in Germany – me and the lads, anyway – whenever we went through a farm. I was good at it. I once killed a pig with a sledge hammer, crept up behind it through all the muck with my boots around my neck, then let smash. It didn't even know what happened. Brained it, first go.' He was so lit up by his own story that the chicken flapped out of his grasp, heading for the gate. Bert, knife in hand, dived from the step and gripped it firm: 'Here you are, Dave. Get it out of its misery.'

Dave forced the neck on to a half-brick, and cut through neatly, ending a crescendo of noise. Blood swelled over the back of his hand, his nose twitching at the smell of it. Then he looked up, grinning at his pair of brothers: 'You thought I'd need some help, did you?' He laughed, head back, grizzled wire hair softening in the atmosphere of slowly descending mist: 'You can come out now, mam. It's all done.' But she stayed wisely by the fire.

Blood seeped between his fingers, making the whole palm sticky, the back of his hand wet and freezing in bitter air. They wanted to get back inside, to the big fruit pie and tea, and the pale blinding fire that gave you spots before the eyes if you gazed at it too long. Dave looked at the twitching rump, his mouth narrow, grey eyes considering, unable to believe it was over so quickly. A feather, minute and beautiful so that he followed it up as far as possible with his eyes, spun and settled on his nose. He didn't fancy knocking it off with the knife-hand. 'Bert, flick it away, for Christ's sake!'

The chicken humped under his sticky palm and hopped its way to a corner of the yard. 'Catch it,' Dave called, 'or it'll fly back home. It's tomorrow's dinner.'

'I can't,' Bert screamed. He'd done so a minute ago, but it was a different matter now, to catch a hen on the rampage with no head.

It tried to batter a way through the wooden door of the lavatory. Dave's well-studded boots slid along the asphalt, and his bones thumped down hard, laying him flat on his back. Full of strength, spirit and decision, it trotted up his chest and on to his face, scattering geranium petals of blood all over his best white shirt. Bert's quick hands descended, but it launched itself from Dave's forehead and off towards the footscraper near the back door. Colin fell on it, unable to avoid its wings spreading sharply into his eyes before doubling away.

Dave swayed on his feet. 'Let's get it quick.' But three did not make a circle, and it soared over its own head and the half-brick of its execution, and was off along the pock-marked yard. You never knew which way it would dive or zigzag. It avoided all hands with uncanny skill, fighting harder now for its life than when it still had a head left to fight for and think with: it was as if the head a few feet away was transmitting accurate messages of warning and direction that it never failed to pick up, an unbreakable line of communication while blood still went through its veins and heart. When it ran over a crust of bread Colin almost expected it to bend its neck and peck at it.

'It'll run down in a bit, like an alarm clock,' Dave said, blood over his trousers, coat torn at the elbow, 'then we'll get the bleeder.' As it ran along the yard the grey December day was stricken by an almost soundless clucking, only half-hearted, as if from miles away, yet tangible nevertheless, maybe a diminution of its earlier protests.

The door of the next house but one was open, and when Bert saw the hen go inside he was on his feet and after it. Dave ran too, the sudden thought striking him that maybe it would shoot out of the front door as well and get run over by a trolley-bus on Wilford Road. It seemed still to have a brain and mind of its own, determined to elude them after its uncalled-for treatment at their hands. They all entered the house without thinking to knock, hunters in a state of ecstasy at having cornered their prey at last, hardly separated from the tail of the hen.

Kitchen lights were full on, a fire in the contemporary-style grate, with Mr Grady at that moment panning more coal on to it. He was an upright hardworking man who lived out his life in overtime on the building sites, except for the treat of his Sunday tea. His wife was serving food to their three grown kids and a couple of relations. She dropped the plate of salmon and screamed as the headless chicken flew up on to the table, clearly on a last bound of energy, and began to spin crazily over plates and dishes. She stared at the three brothers in the doorway.

'What is it? Oh dear God, what are you doing? What is it?'

Mr Grady stood, a heavy poker in his hand, couldn't speak while the animal reigned over his table, continually hopping and taking-off, dropping blood and feathers, its webbed feet scratching silently over butter and trifle, the soundless echo of clucking seeming to come from its gaping and discontinued neck.

Dave, Bert and Colin were unable to move, stared as it stamped circle-wise over bread and jelly, custard and cress. Colin was somehow expecting Mr Grady to bring down the poker and end this painful and ludicrous situation – in which the hen looked like beating them at last.

It fell dead in the salad, greenery dwarfed by snowing feathers and flecks of blood. The table was wrecked, and the reality of his ruined, hard-earned tea-party reached Mr Grady's sensitive spot. His big face turned red, after the whiteness of shock and superstitious horror. He fixed his wild eyes on Dave, who drew back, treading into his brothers' ankles:

'You bastards,' Grady roared, poker still in hand and watched by all. 'You bastards, you!'

'I'd like my chicken back,' Dave said, as calmly as the sight of Grady's face and shattered table allowed.

Bert and Colin said nothing. Dave's impetuous thieving had never brought them anything but trouble, as far as they could remember – now that things had gone wrong. All this trouble out of one chicken.

Grady girded himself for the just answer: 'It's *my* chicken now,' he said, trying to smile over it.

'It ain't,' Dave said, obstinate.

'You sent it in on purpose,' Grady cried, half tearful again, his great chest heaving. 'I know you lot, by God I do. Anything for devilment.'

'I'd like it back.'

Grady's eyes narrowed, the poker higher. 'Get away from my house.'

'I'm not going till I've got my chicken.'

'Get out.' He saw Dave's mouth about to open in further argument, but Grady was set on the ultimate word – or at least the last one that mattered, under the circumstances. He brought the poker down on the dead chicken, cracking the salad bowl, a gasp from everyone in the room, including the three brothers. 'You should keep your animals under control,' he raved. 'I'm having this. Now put yourselves on the right side of my doorstep or I'll split every single head of you.'

That final thump of the poker set the full stop on all of them, as if the deathblow had been Grady's and gave him the last and absolute right over it. They retreated. What else could you do in face of such barbarity? Grady had always had that sort of reputation. It would henceforth stick with him, and he deserved it more than ever. They would treat him accordingly.

Dave couldn't get over his defeat and humiliation – and his loss that was all the more bitter since the hen had come to him so easily. On their way to the back door he was crying: 'I'll get that fat bleeding navvy. What a trick to play on somebody who lives in the same yard! I'll get the bastard. He'll pay for that chicken. By God he will. He's robbed a man of his dinner. He won't get away with a thing like that.'

But they were really thinking about what they were going to say to their mother, who had stayed in the house, and who would no doubt remind them for the next few weeks that there was some justice left in the world, and that for the time being it was quite rightly on the side of Mr Grady.

CANALS

WHEN Dick received the letter saying his father hadn't long to live he put a black tie in his pocket, got leave from the school where he taught, and took the first train up.

In a tunnel his face was reflected clearly, brown eyes shadowed underneath from the pressure of a cold that had been trying to break out but that his will-power still held back. He considered that there had never been a good photograph taken of him, certainly none reflecting the fine image he saw when looking in the mirror of the thin-faced, hard, sensitive man whose ancestors must all have had similar bones and features. But photographs showed him weak, a face that couldn't retain its strength at more than one angle, and that people might look at and not know whether this uncertainty was mere charm or a subtle and conscious form of deception. He had a wide mouth and the middling forehead of a practical man whose highest ambition was, once upon a time, to be a good tool-setter, until he joined the army and discovered that he was intelligent in a more worldly sense. And when he left he knew that he would never go into a factory again.

In his briefcase were a shirt and two handkerchiefs his wife had forced on him at the last moment, as well as a razor, and some magazines scooped up in case he had nothing to think about on the journey.

Sitting in the dining-car for lunch, alone yet surrounded by many people, he remembered his mother saying, when he was leaving home ten years before:

'Well, you'll always be able to come back. If you can't come home again, where can you go?' But on a visit after four years he walked into the house and, apart from a brief hello, nobody turned from the television set to greet him, though they'd been a close-blooded family, and on and off the best of friends all their lives.

So he never really went back, didn't see himself as the sort of person who ever would. Whether he ever went forward or not was another question, but he certainly knew there was no profit in looking back. He preferred a new block of flats to a cathedral any day, a good bus-service to a Rembrandt or historic ruin, though he realized it was better to have *all* these things and not be in the position of having to choose.

He remembered his father saying: 'A good soldier never looks back. He don't even polish the backs of his boots. You can see your face in the toecaps, though.' His father had never been a soldier, yet this was his favourite saying – because he'd never been forward anywhere, either.

So the only time he did go back was when his father was dying. It wasn't a question of having to, or even thinking about it: he just went, stayed for a week while his father died and got buried, then came back, leaving his mother in charge of brothers and sisters, even though he was the eldest son.

He stayed with his father day and night for three days, except when he queued for pills at the all-night chemist's downtown. He felt there was no need to make a song-and-dance about anyone dying, even your own father, because you should have done that while they were alive. He hoped he'd get better, yet knew he wouldn't. At fifty-four a lavish and royal grip of rottenness that refused to let go had got him in the head, a giant invisible cancerous rat with the dullest yet most tenacious teeth in the world, pressing its way through that parchment skull. He sweated to death, died at a quarter to five in the afternoon, and no one had ever told him he was going to die.

His mother didn't shed a tear. She was afraid of death and of her husband, hated him with reason because he had always without intending it turned her on to the monstrous path of having no one to hate but herself. She had hardly been in to see him during the last three days, and neither had his two daughters. Dick and his brother held each other in an embrace, two grown men unable to stop themselves sobbing like children.

A young thin woman of the neighbourhood laid the father out, and Dick went to get the doctor, who filled in a death-certificate without bothering to come and see that his patient had actually died.

The undertakers took him away. The mattress was rolled up and put outside for the dustbin men. Then the bed he'd laid on was folded back into a settee, making the small room look empty – all within an hour of him dying. An aunt who'd also lost her husband hadn't shed a tear either. Maybe it runs in the family, he thought. At the funeral, walking from the house to the waiting car, his mother wept for the first and last time – in front of all the neighbours. Of his father's five brothers none came to see him off, though all knew of it. It was almost as if he'd died in the middle of a battlefield, there were so few witnesses. But at least he didn't know about it, and might not have worried much if he had. And who am I to talk? Dick wondered, much later. I never went back to his grave, and I doubt if anyone else did, either. His mother's lack of tears didn't strike him as strange at the time considering the life she and their father had led.

Between the death and burial he was nut-loose and roaming free. At first, the brothers, sisters and mother went out together in the evenings, sticking close in a single corner of a bar-room snug, not talking except to stand up and ask who wanted what. Once they went to the pictures, but afterwards drifted into their separate ways.

It was early May, and all he wanted to do was walk. The low small sky of the bedroom ceiling had turned to blue, white angels and angles of cloud shifting across between factory and house skyline. It was vast above, and made the streets look even smaller. He hated them, wished a fire-tailed rocket would spin from the sky and wash them clean with all-enduring phosphorus. He was thirty-three, and old enough to know better than wish for that, or to think it would come when he wanted it to, or that it would make any difference if ever it did.

The greatest instinct is to go home again, the unacknowledged urge of the deracinated, the exiles – even when it isn't admitted. The only true soul is the gipsy's, and he takes home and family with him wherever he drifts. The nomad pushes his roots about like the beetle his ball of dung, lives on what he scavenges from the rock and sand of the desert. It's a good man or woman who evades it and is not poisoned precisely because he has avoided it while knowing all about it. You take on the soul of the Slav, and if you can eventually find that sort of soul it falls around you like a robe and makes you feel like a king. The wandering Jew carried the secret of creation in the pocket of his long overcoat, and now he has ploughed it into the fields of Israel. The Siberian nomad has formed his collective or joined a work-gang on some giant dam that will illuminate the wilderness his ancestors were free to wander in. Is the desert then all that is left? If the houses and factories stretching for miles around are a desert for one's soul, then maybe the desert itself is the Garden of Eden, even if one dries up and dies in it.

But he knew at the same time that life had two sides, and a base-line set firmly on the earth. The good air was blowing through the fresh-leafed trees of the cemetery he was passing. There was moss between the sandstone lumps of the wall, well bedded and livid where most damp had got at it. Between spring and summer there was a conscious feeling to the year, a mellow blight of reminiscence and nostalgia blending with the softening sweet air of late afternoon. The atmosphere made buildings and people stand out clearly, as if the meadow-and-water clouds of the Trent had not dispersed and still held that magical quality of light while passing high over the hills and roof-tops of the city. It was a delight to be alive and walking, and for some reason he wanted the day to go on for ever. There was a terrible beauty in the city he belonged to that he had never found anywhere else.

He walked over Bobber's Mill bridge, far enough out to smell soil of allotment gardens, loam of fields, water of the mill-racing Leen that had streamed down from beyond Newstead. In spite of petrol, the reek of upholstery, and fag-smoke coming from a bus-door when it stopped near him, he held on to this purity of vision that made him believe life was good and worth living.

He walked by the railway bank and through the allotment gardens – still exactly there from fifteen years ago. Feeling himself too old to be indulging in such fleshly reminiscence, he enjoyed it all the more, not as a vice but as if it were food to a starving man. Every elm tree, oak tree, apple tree, lime tree represented a leaning-post for kisses, a pausing place to talk and rest at, light cigarettes, wait while Marian fastened her coat or put on more lipstick. Every wooden gateway in the tall hedges that were as blind as walls brought to mind the self-indulgent embraces and love-making of his various courting mates. Different generations of thrushes were still loud in the same tree-tops, hawthorn, and privet, except that their notes and noise were more exactly the same.

The brook was as usual stagnant, yet water came from somewhere, green button-eyed weed making patterns on the surface to blot out cloud reflections and blue sky. Tadpoles had passed away, and young frogs were jumping under the unreachable part of the hedge. To observe all this, connect it to his past life and give it no part in his future, made him feel an old man, certainly far older than he was. Maybe he was merely mature, when what you saw and thought about no longer drove you on to the next action of your life no matter how small that action turned out to be.

The uterine flight of reminiscence, the warm piss of nostalgia as he stood by a hedge and relieved himself where the shaded pathway stretched emptily in both directions, was a way of filling in the void that a recent death created, especially the death of a person whose life had been utterly unfulfilled – of which there are so many, and which makes you feel it deeply because on the watershed of such sorrow you sense that your life too could turn out at the end to have been equally unfulfilled. The vital breezes of clean air shaking the hedgetops don't let such thoughts stay long. The lack of your own persistence in real life is often bad, while the lack of it in self-destroying thoughts at such times as this is occasionally good.

The canal had dried up, been dammed and drained

and in places built over. In the mouldering soft colour of dusk he walked from one bank to another. The old stone bridge had been allowed to drop into the canal below and fill it in, hump and all, and a white-lined and tarmacked road had been laid straight across it.

He followed what was left, walked along its old towpath towards the country. A large open pond lay down to the right with indistinct banks except for a scrap of wood on the western side now touched by a barleycorn dip of the sun. A smell of raw smoke and water was wafted in his direction. The headstocks of the colliery where his grandfather had worked blocked off an opposite view, and it was so close that the noise of turbines and generators made a fitting counterpoint to reawakening senses.

It was dark by the time he stepped into the Ramrod and Musket and ordered a pint of beer. A fire burned in one of the side rooms, and he sat by it, loosening his raincoat. Everyone he saw he felt pity for. The wells of it had not stopped pumping, and the light of it was too blinding for him to turn it round on himself, a beam he alone could explore the world with, prise it from the darkness it lived in. He had come here thinking he might meet someone known from years ago, though he would never acknowledge such a lapse in case its nerve-racking mixture of pride and weakness might poison all hope in him.

Going outside to the back, there was no bulb in the socket to light his way. Indigo had faded completely from the sky, and he stepped slowly across the yard with eyes shut tight, under the illusion that he could see better than if he walked with them open and arms held out for fear of colliding with something.

The liquid in his pint went down, a spiritual nilometer latched by the river of his momentarily stilled life. He felt comfortable, hearing the homely accents of the few other men dealing out chitchat that in London he wouldn't give tuppence for. Nostalgia was sweet, and he allowed it to seep into him with a further jar of beer. The others sat back from the fire, glasses set on labelled mats, sliding them around to make a point.

He hated beer after the third pint, a senseless waterlogging of the body that adiposed it to the earth one tried to get away from. He thought of going on to another place when no one came in that he knew, but considered a pub-crawl futile – except that the ground covered between them is different and shakes the stuff to a lower level to make room for more. Otherwise stay at the first one you stumble into.

The more he drank the more his cold bothered him. Death and the funeral had held it off, but now it spread the poison and colour of infection, a slight shifting of every feature from its spot-on proportion in order to recoup the truth and clarity of things past. One's feelings were important during a cold, in showing what you are really like and what stirs your mind from one decade to the next. It was almost as if the real you was a reactionary because it rooted you so firmly to the past without calling on detail as a support, giving it the slightly sick air which all reactionaries must have as a permanent condition. In so many cases the only key to the past is sentimentality – unless one has that cold or sickness which puts it in its place. He had reviled the past, but to loathe something was the first step to understanding it, just as to love something was the first step towards abandoning it. The past is a cellar, twisting catacombs or filled-in canals, but a cellar in which you have to walk in order to put a bullet into the back of the head of whatever monarch may be ruling too autocratically there. Only you have to tread slowly, warily, to make sure you get the right one, because if by any chance you get the wrong one you might end up putting a bullet into the back of your own head.

He was married, and had three children, one of them a few weeks old, so that his wife had not been able to come up from London with him. It was years since he had been so alone, and it was like a new experience, which he did not quite know how to handle, or realize what might come of it. People so alone rarely had chance meetings, yet the day after his father had died, walking across the city centre on his way to register the death, he heard someone from the roof-tops calling his name.

He didn't think he was hearing things, or going mad, because it was not in his nature to do so. His physical build seemed absolutely to preclude it. But he stopped, looked, then felt foolish at having been mistaken. It was a fine, blustery Nottingham day, with green double-decker buses almost surrounding the market square, and a few people actually crossing the road.

'Dick!' The voice came again, but he walked away since it was obviously some workman shouting to his mate. 'Dick! Dick!' The voice was closer, so he stopped to light a cigarette in case it really wasn't meant for him.

His cousin came scurrying down a series of ladders and dropped on the pavement a few yards away. He was, as the saying goes, 'all over him' — they hadn't met for so long, and had been such close friends, born on the same fish day of March, a wild blizzarding day in which no fish had a chance of swimming.

Bernard was thin and wiry, even through the old jacket and trousers of a builder's labourer. His grey eyes were eager with friendship, and they embraced on the street: 'I didn't know you was in Nottingham,' he said fussily. 'Why didn't you write and tell me? Fancy meeting like this.' He laughed about it, seeing himself as having climbed down from the sky like a monkey.

'I came up all of a sudden. How did you recognize me from right up there?'

'Your face. And that walk. I'd know it anywhere.'

'Dad was ill. He died last night.'

'Uncle Joe?' he took off his cap, pushed back fair and matted hair in the wind, bewildered at the enormity of the event and, Dick thought, at not being able to say anything about it.

'He had cancer.'

There was a pub near by: 'Let's go for a drink,' Bernard said.

'Won't the foreman mind?'

'I expect so. Come on. They've had enough sweat out of me. I'm sorry Joe died.'

They sat in the otherwise empty bar. 'Come up and see us all before you go back,' he said. 'We'd be glad if you would. I don't know what you live in London for, honest I don't. There's plenty of schools you could teach at in Nottingham. They're crying out for teachers, I'll bet. I suppose it's a bit of a dump, but you can't beat it. At least I don't reckon so.'

'It's all right,' Dick said, 'but London's where I belong – if I belong anywhere.' They talked as if it were on the other side of the world, which it was against the background of their common memories – even further.

'Well, you can't beat the town you were brought up in – dragged up, I mean!' Bernard said. Dick remembered, and talked about it before he could stop himself, of when they were children, and he and Bernard used to go around houses asking for old rags and scrap, which they would then sell for picture-money and food. The houses whose gardens backed on to the recreation ground were somewhat better off than the ones they lived in, and therefore good for pickings. At one a youngish woman gave them bread and jam and cups of tea, which they gladly accepted. They didn't call often, and not many others went around to spoil their pitch. And yet, good as she was, sweet as the tea and jam tasted, they couldn't keep going there. There was some slight feeling of shame about it, probably quite unjustified, yet picked up by both of them all the same. Without even saying anything to each other they stopped calling. Dick wondered what the woman had thought, and whether she had missed them.

Though he remembered this common incident clearly, it soon became obvious that Bernard did not, and that his mind was a blank regarding it, though at first he had looked as if he did vaguely recollect it, and then as if he wanted to but couldn't quite pull it back. 'Still,' Dick said, laughing it away, 'you can't go home again, I know that.'

'You can't?' Bernard asked, full of surprise. 'Why can't you?'

'I can't, anyway.'

'You can do what you like, can't you?'

'Some people can.'

They drank to it.

'Bring your wife and kids here to live. Get a house up Sherwood Rise. It's healthy there. They'll love it.'

'I can't, because I don't want to.'

He laughed. 'Maybe you are better off down there, at that. I can't trap yo' into owt. I'm sorry about Uncle Joe though; Mam'll be upset when I tell her.'

'It'll be in the paper today.'

'She'll see it, then. Let me get you one now.'

'Next time. I must be off.'

Dick watched him ascend the ladders, up from the

pavement to the first storey, then to the second. From the roof he straddled a parapet, turned and looked down, a gargoyle for one moment, then he took off his cap and waved, a wide frantic smile on his far-off face. Dick had time to wave back before he leapt up and was hidden by a chimney-stack.

The past is like a fire – don't put your hand in it. And yet, what is to stop you walking through it upright, all of you, body and soul? It was a weekday, and the pub hadn't filled up. Near to ten o'clock he couldn't bear the thought of going home. His impulse was to flee towards London, but he'd promised to stay on a few days. It was expected of him, and for once in his life he had to obey.

He'd called here often for a drink with Marian, though she'd always insisted on having her shandy outside because she wasn't yet eighteen, as if it would have made much difference. After a summer's night on Bramcote Hills the thirst was killing, and he drank more beer in those days than he could ever stomach now. The good food of London living had peppered his gut with ulcers – or so it felt, without having been to any doctor – and the heartburn was sure to grip him next day if he put back too much.

The last bus was at half past ten, and he thought he might as well walk home. Outside, fastening his coat in the lighted doorway, the insane idea came to call on Marian, to go down to the estate and knock on her door. Why think about it, if you intended doing it? The one advantage of dwelling on the past was to act without thought if you were to get the utmost from it. In that way, of course, it would end up getting the utmost out of you, but that was nothing to be afraid of.

Fifteen years was a long time, judging by the excitement the hope of meeting her again let loose in him. It was similar to that when they had been 'going out' with each other for what seemed a decade, but which had not felt much like being in love at the time.

Having started factory work at fourteen, he was a seasoned man by the age of eighteen, and those four years had slowed down to become the longest in his life, possibly because there was an end to them which he hadn't foreseen at the time. In them, he grew up and died. His courtships had seemed eternal, even when they only lasted several months – looking back on them. The time with Marian went on longest of all, and being the last it was also the most important in that microcosmic life.

A fine drizzle powdered across the orange sodium lights of the housing estate. The roads were just as wide as he'd remembered them. If so little alters in a man's life, who but the most bigoted can believe in progress? Such a question came, he knew, of having too little faith, and of too complete immersion in a past so far away and severed that it couldn't be anything else but irrelevant fiction. Yet it didn't feel like it, and it did not disturb him that it didn't. The familiar dank smell of coal-smoke hovered even along the wide avenues and crescents, and the closeness of his cigarette tasted the same in his mouth and nostrils as it had all those years ago. Privet hedges shone with water under the streetlamps, and a well-caped railwayman rode by on a bicycle that seemed to have no light until only a yard away. He pulled up by the kerb, and the latch clattered as he went up the path and round to his own back door.

It was a good distance, yet he wished it were longer, both because he was apprehensive at meeting Marian and because it would spin out further the pleasant anticipation of her being at home. She'd been going with his friend Barry when he first met her, a carnal and passionate love similar to the one he at the time was pursuing with someone else. But Barry went into the army, driven from home by a black-haired bossy mother and a house full of sisters, lit off at seventeen into the Engineers just as the war ended. Letters and the occasional leave were no way to keep love's fires stoked between him and Marian, and one night Dick met her by chance and, on seeing her home, fell into honeyed and violent kisses by her gate. She agreed to see him again, and he didn't realize to what extent he had run his mate off until Barry clocked on with the army for twelve years and went straight off to Greece to serve two of them. They even stayed friends over it, yet the blow to Barry had been hard, as he admitted when they met, years later.

He made up his mind to turn at the next corner and go home, to leave the past in its matchwood compartment and not smash over it with the bulldozer of his useless and idiotic obsession. She would be out, or a husband would meet him at the door and tell him he'd got the wrong house. He smiled to remember how, during the war, an American soldier had called one night on the woman next door, as had been his habit for some months. But this time his opening of the door was answered by the husband, who had unexpectedly finished his stint on nights. The American stared unbelievingly at the pudgy and belligerent face. After a few seconds he backed out with the lame remark, 'Sorry, I thought it was a public house.' The husband had accepted it as a genuine mistake, but there were some snide comments going around the street for a long time on how lucky Mrs So-and-so was to have such a numbskull for a husband. So if Marian's husband was at home, or some man she might be living with, he'd merely say: 'Is Mrs Smith in?' and make some excuse about getting the number of the house wrong.

Having decided to go home and not be such a fool, he kept on his track towards Marian's as if locked in some deep and serpentine canal, unable to scale its side and get back to sane air. He even went more quickly, without feeling or thought or sense of direction. From the public house he had forgotten the exact streets to follow, but it didn't matter, for he simply walked looking mostly towards the ground, recognizing the shadows of a bus-shelter, the precise spot reached by the spreading rays of a particular street-lamp, the height of a kerb, or twitchel posts at the end of a cul-de-sac.

He found the road and the number, opened the gate, and walked down the path with even more self-assurance than he ever had after courting her for a year. There was a light on in the living room. The fifteen years had not been a complete blank. He'd heard that her mother had died and that she had married a man who had been sent to prison and whom she had refused to see again. Barry also told him that there had been one child, a son. The first five years after they split up must have been agony to her, blow after blow, and it was as if he were going back now to see how she had borne the suffering that followed in his wake. But no, he could never admit to so much power. He stood at the back door, in darkness for some minutes, torn at last by the indecision that should have gripped him on his way there, and splintered by the remorse he might feel after he had left. The noise of a television set came from inside, music and crass speech that made it impossible to tell whether one or a dozen people were at home.

He too had gone into the army, and when her letters grew less frequent he was almost glad at the sense of freedom he felt. But her thoughts and feelings were not of the sort she could put easily in writing and transmit that way, as he found when they met on his first leave. Passion, because it was incommunicable, was her form of love. It was fully flowered and would go on forever with regard to him, incapable of development yet utterly complete. He expected letters, subtlety, variation, words, words, words, and couldn't stand the emptiness of such fulfilment. She could foresee no greater happiness than that they get married, and would have demanded little more than the most basic necessities of life. If he had been a man he would have accepted this, because he also loved her; and if he were a man now he would not have come back looking for her, unable to say what he wanted, whether it was love or chaos he hoped to resurrect.

It was no use standing in the dark with such thoughts, so he knocked at the door. She opened it, set up the two steps in an oblong of pale orange light. 'What do you want?' she said, seeing only a stranger and at this time of night. The protective voice of a boy called from inside:

'Who is it, Mam?'

Regret, indecision, dread had gone, for he had acted, had the deepest instincts of his heart carried out for him, which really meant that he had been acted upon. He smiled, telling her who it was.

She repeated his name, and looked closer, eyes narrowing almost to a squint, 'You! Fancy you!'

'Well,' he said, 'I was passing and thought I'd see if you still lived here.'

She asked him in, and they stood in the small kitchen. He saw it was painted white instead of cream, had an electric stove in place of the old gas one, but with the same sink now patched and stained.

'Who is it, Mam?'

'I'm surprised you still knew where I lived.'

'I don't suppose I could ever forget it. In any case it's not that long ago.'

'No? It is, though.'

'It doesn't feel like it to me.'

But, to look at her, it was. And she was thinking the same. She seemed taller, was more full-bodied, no longer the pale, slim, wildlife girl of eighteen. The set lines running from her mouth, which he remembered as being formed by that curious smile of wanting to know something more definite and significant about what had caused her to smile in the first place, had hardened and deepened because her curiosity hadn't been responded to, and because the questions could never be formed clearly enough in her to ask them. The smile had moved to the grey eyes, and was more forthright in its limitations, less expressive but no longer painful.

'Come in,' she said. 'I'll make you a cup of tea, if you'd like one.'

'All right. I will for a minute.' Once inside he forgot his absence and hesitancy and took off his coat. Her twelve-year-old son lay as far back as he could get in an armchair, watching television from too close by, a livid perpetual lightning flicker to Dick, who wasn't facing it. His mother made him turn it down. 'This is Peter,' she said. 'Peter, this is an old friend of your Mam's.'

Peter said nothing, an intelligent face blighted by sudden resentment at another man in the house. He looked harder into the telly in case his mother should ask him to turn it right off. Marian's hands shook as she poured the tea, put in sugar and milk. 'I can't get over it,' she said, 'you coming to see me. Of all people! Do you know anybody else around here?'

'Nobody. Only you.'

She was happy at the thought that he had come especially to see her. 'You haven't altered much in all these years.'

'Neither have you.'

Her ironic grin was the same: 'Not much I haven't! You can't lie to me any more. You did once though, didn't you, duck?'

He might have done, and the fact that he'd forgotten was made to seem unforgivable by the slight shock still on her face at his sudden reappearance. Still, she managed to laugh about the thought of him having lied to her once, though he knew better than to take such laughs at their face value. 'Did you come up by car?' she asked. 'What sort is it?'

'I don't have a car.'

'I thought you would have. Then you could have taken me and Peter for a ride in it some time. Couldn't he, Peter?'

A 'yes' broke from the back of Peter's mind. 'You know,' she said, 'when I heard you'd become a schoolteacher I had to see the funny side of it. Fancy me going out for so long with a man who was going to become a schoolteacher! No wonder you chucked somebody like me up. I don't blame you, though.'

'That wasn't why I chucked you up. If I did.'

'You might have done – anyway,' she reflected.

'I don't remember who chucked who up.'

'You loved me though, didn't you?' She said this so that Peter wouldn't hear, from within the clatter and shouting of his private gunfight.

'I did,' he answered.

'You said you wanted to stay in the army for good, and so getting married wouldn't be fair to either of us. I remember all of it clearly. But I could see that that wasn't it at all, though. You'd just lost interest. There was nowt else you could get to know about me, after all the times we had. We didn't even fall out with each other. I didn't know what to tell the girls at work when they asked about you.'

Every word and nuance of her recollected past was accurate. It was no use saying he was only eighteen at the time, because he (as well as she) held himself totally responsible for his actions. Four years at work made him man enough already, and it wasn't so much shame he felt now as a failure of masculine responsibility. Yet some innate and ruthless sense had steered him from a life he was unfitted for. She spoke as if it were last year, whereas to him it was a whole lifetime ago, and could be considered in one way as the immature skirt-chasing of a callow youth, and in another as the throwback past of a man who, being incapable of forgetting it, had been unable to grow up. And if, beyond all this, he had stepped from one world and settled himself securely in another with a wife, three children, and an all-absorbing job, why had he made this painful and paranoid expedition to the world he had launched out from? His age didn't justify it. Maybe in his deracinated life he was forgetting where he had come from, yet wasn't a visit home enough to remind him? One had to make journeys in all directions, was the only answer that came while listening to Marian. Happy are those who don't make journeys and never need to, he thought, yet luckier are those who do.

Peter had gone to bed, more willingly than he expected. He opened a half-bottle of whisky bought in the pub, and Marian set out two glasses: 'To you and your life,' he said.

'To yourn,' she answered. 'I hardly ever drink, but this tastes good for a change. It might buck me up.' She sat on the sofa they had made love on countless times, and he stayed on a straight-backed chair at the table on which plates, cups, and sauce-bottle still rested. A clothes-horse barricaded the fire from them.

'I work at the same place still,' she said, 'at the stocking factory. I've got a better job now, though: I fault them, prick them under a glass so that they won't last more than three months. It's a good job, faulting. I can make twelve pounds a week on piecework. It's hard though in wintertime, because I go to work on my bike, riding up the hill with a January wind hitting me head-on. I went on a bus once, but halfway there the driver had a dizzy spell. He turned round, shouting for everybody to jump off, before he was able to stop it. The only time I ever went on the bus, as well! Everything happens to me!'

'What was this I heard about your husband?' he asked, noticing the regularity of her teeth. All were false, and none of his had come out yet.

'Him?' she said. 'Oh, when you left me I got married a year later. I met him at a dance, and never realized he was no good. Not long after we were married, while Mam was still alive – though on that morning she'd gone out shopping, thank God, or she'd have died at the shock I'm sure – I was in here washing up when two policemen knocked at the back door and asked if Arthur Baldwin lived here. I felt my heart going like mad, pitter-patter, and thought he'd been run over or killed in a machine at work, ready for the tears to burst out of me. But it wasn't that at all. They'd picked him up on the street because they'd found out he'd been breaking into houses, and I don't know what else he'd done. I didn't go to court, and never even read the papers about it. In fact he hadn't been at work for a long time, and I thought he had. I was such a baby I never realized what was going on. He'd been in trouble with the police before we met, but I didn't know anything about it, and nobody thought to tell me. He'd even got another woman he was keeping, in the Meadows. His mother asked me to go down to the court and plead for him, because I was pregnant already, but I didn't. I wouldn't have anything to do with it. "He's got hisself into it," I told her, "so he can get hisself out of it." She threatened me, but I still wouldn't do it, and then my mother nearly threw her out of the house. It wouldn't have helped much, anyway, I know that, because the police had really got it in for him, just as I had as well for the way he'd done it on me.

'He was sent to prison for two years, and I haven't seen him since. As I say, I was pregnant, and Peter was born while he was in prison. He don't know anything about it yet, though he'll have a right to some day. I just tell him that his father left me when he was a baby. Mam and me got a bed down from upstairs when I had Peter, and fixed it up in this corner, and I had him on it. Then a year later Mam went, and I've lived alone ever since, the last ten years. I wouldn't get married again now, though, not for a fortune. All I've got is Peter, and it's enough for me, bringing him up. He's a bit of a handful at times, being without a dad, but when he is he gets my fist. Mind you, we have some good times together as well. We go fishing now and again, and he loves it, sitting by the canal with all his tackle and bait, net and floats. He feels a proper man, and I don't mind buying him the best stuff to do it with. He's very clever though at mechanical things. All he does is build things up. He's got all sorts of radio kits and construction sets. I never have to touch a fuse: he mends them all. He fixed a transistor radio last week for Mrs Barnes next door, and she was ever so pleased. She gave him ten bob.

'I work hard, so we live well. Last year we rented a

caravan at Cleethorpes with the couple next door, and stayed a fortnight. I look a sight in a bathing costume, but we went swimming every day, and had a marvellous time. Mr Barnes got a car and we went all over Lincolnshire picnicking. It won't be all that long now before Peter starts work, and then he'll be bringing in some money as well. He doesn't want to stay on at school, at least he says he don't, though I don't think he'll be able to change his mind if he decides to.

'I suppose it was hardest for me though when Mam went. It was cancer, but she wasn't badly for very long. She never went to bed, stopped going when she knew she was going to die, though nobody told her, just lay on this sofa at night and sat in that armchair during the day. I don't know how we managed with just each other. I knew she was going to die, and that when she went there'd be no one left. Then I'd hear Peter crying, and knew that there would be, but it didn't make much difference for a long time. Still, we've all got to go, though it don't do to think about it.'

'We're young yet,' Dick said. 'We're just over thirty.' He sat by her on the sofa and took her hand. Was it true then that in all the troubles people had, no one could help anyone else, be of much use to soothe and comfort? Was everyone alone in their own black caverns and never communicating by tunnel or canal?

'I had help,' she said. 'The neighbours did what they could. At a time like that only God can help you, and it's only then you realize He can't. We aren't taking a holiday this year. I can't afford it because I got Peter a pickup and tape-recorder. But the year after, if we're still here, we're hoping to go to Norfolk for ten days. Gives us summat to look forward to.'

'I expect you'll get married again one day,' he said.

'Married?' she jeered. 'Not me, mate. I've had my

life. No more kids, either. The woman next door had a baby last week, and when she came in to see me with it I laughed at her for being so quick in her visiting and said: "Hey, don't come in here spreading your feathers!" And she laughed as well, as if it might not be a bad idea, but I knew it worn't. All I want to do is bring Peter up, get him a good start in life. I don't mind working for that, and living for it. I'll work till I drop, but as for getting married, you don't know what I've had to go through. And don't think I'm squealing about it. I might have done at one time, but not any more, because it's all over. I'm not going to get married and have them all come back.'

'You can fall in love, you know.' He detected a weakness in her that she had obviously long brooded on.

'No, I won't.'

'That's what you say now. There's no telling when it'll come.'

'I loved you,' she said, 'and you can only be in love once in your life, the first time. There ain't any other.' Her conviction was quiet, all jeering gone. She pressed his hand, and he leaned over to kiss her on the cheek. 'It's like a dream,' she said, smiling, her eyes shining as if the tears would break. 'You coming back. I can't believe it. I can't, duck, honest I can't.'

She wasn't in love with him, no more than he was with her, but he had lured her into the spider-trap of the past, and she was sweetening within it. 'No,' she said, 'I'll never fall in love.'

'You don't have to be in love to get married,' he said.

'That's what I thought before,' she answered, 'and look what happened.'

'Love is a destroyer if you wait for it too long. If you like somebody, love can come out of it. It's no use wrecking your life for want of being in love. Sometimes I think that as soon as you start talking about love it's on its way out, that really it's nothing more than the bloody relic of a bygone age that civilization no longer needs. There's something wicked and destructive about it.'

'I don't properly understand you,' she said gently, 'but you're wrong, anyway. You're only saying it to soothe me. You don't need to, you know, I'm all right. I'm not as sour as I sound.'

The door opened without warning and Peter appeared in his dressing-gown, eyes blinded by the light as if he'd already been half asleep, though Dick thought he may have been listening to their talk for a while. 'What do you want?' Marian asked.

'I'm looking for my comic.' He found it, under a cushion of the sofa they were sitting on. 'Don't stay up late, duck,' she said. 'You've got to go to school in the morning.'

He stood by the door, looking at them. 'Are you coming to bed then, Mam?'

'Soon. We're just having a talk about old times. I shan't be long.'

He went up the stairs, slowly, drawing the sleeve of his dressing-gown against the wall.

She made more tea, took out a box of photographs and went through them one by one, then got him to empty his wallet and show pictures of his wife and children. The past was impotent, finally, with no cleansing quality in its slow-burning fires. Yet they could never be put out because the canals that led to them were baked dry at the bottom with the rusting and tattered debris of the life you lead.

'I didn't think you'd ever go to live in London, though,' she said. 'It's a long way off.'

'Two hours by train. There and back in half a day. Nothing.'

'Not if you live there, and was born here. Shall you come and see me again?'

He stood up and put on his coat. 'I'd like to, if you won't kick me out.'

'Well, maybe I won't.'

'I don't come up too often, though.'

'It don't matter. We could go to a pub or summat, couldn't we?'

He held her close. 'We could.'

'It don't matter though, if you don't want to. But come in and see me.'

'All right, love.'

They held each other close, and kissed for a few seconds, standing near the kitchen door. 'I can't believe it,' she said. 'I still can't. Why did you come back? Why?' He couldn't say. He didn't know. The fifteen years fizzled down to nothing. It wasn't that he'd been a man at eighteen. He was a youth, and the raging sweet waves of it crushed into him, two flat heads of vice-steel closing with nothing in between.

'What did you say?' he asked.

'Nothing. I didn't way owt.' He kissed the tears out of her eyes.

After midnight he walked through fire, tattered and burned, going the same track home as on the hundreds of occasions when he had stayed late and missed his bus, blinded and blindfolded across the wide roads and by the black hedge-bound footpath of Collier's Pad. Only the train might take him out of it.

Lights crouched in the distance all around, every tree-root holy, the foliage damned. The narrow path was hedged in by uncertainty and chaos, life's way spun out of suffering and towards death. Artificially lighted air blighted your lungs, and you now and again stopped on your walk by some half-concealed bran-tub to dip your hands into the entrails of the past when destruction wasn't coming on you fast enough; the past is only good when what you pull up can be seen as part of the future.

But his heart was full of Marian's fate, up to her death and his death, and he felt better in knowing that at least they had this much in common whether they saw each other again or not.

THE ROAD

WHEN Ivan was five his parents took him on a day-trip to Skegness. They wanted to spend a few hours out of the city and see the coast where they had languished for ten days of a misty frustrating honeymoon of long ago, but Stanley said: 'Let's take Ivan to the seaside. It'll do him good.'

'Yes,' his mother said. 'He'll love it.'

And Ivan, sucking a lollipop as they walked up Arkwright Street, was oblivious to the responsibility they had put on to his shoulders. Yesterday the car had broken down, so they were going by train. To Stanley everything always happened at the crucial moment, otherwise why did it happen at all?

Ivan wore a new navy blazer, and long trousers specially creased for Whitsun. His shoes were polished and tight around his checked socks. Dark thin hair was well parted, and shy blue eyes looked out of a pale face that tapered from a broad forehead down to his narrow chin and royal blue tie. He held his father with one hand, and gripped his lollipop with the other.

'It'll be marvellous to get to the sea,' Stanley said. 'It's a hard life being a waiter, and good to have a whole day off for a change.'

Amy agreed on all counts, though didn't say so aloud. Ivan wondeered if there'd be boats, and she answered that she dare say there would be. Stanley picked Ivan up and put him high on his shoulders: 'We'd better hurry.'

'You'll have a heart attack if you're not careful,' she laughed. 'Like in them adverts!'

'We've got to get going, though.'

'There's still half an hour,' she said, 'and we're nearly there.' Such bleak and common rush seemed to expose her more to the rigours of the world than was necessary, so she would never run, not even for a bus that might make her late for work if she missed it. But then, she never was late for work, and it was part of Stanley's job to get a move on.

He fought his way into the carriage to get seats, and even then Amy had to sit a few rows down. Ivan stayed with his father, now and again standing on his grey flannel trousers for a better view. The carriage was full, and he adjusted quickly to his new home, for all the unfamiliar people in the compartment became part of his family. Strange faces that he would be half afraid of on the street or in dreams seemed now so close and large and smiling, loud in their gaze or talk, that they could not but be uncles and aunts and cousins. In which case he could look with absolute safety at everything outside.

His blue eyes pierced with telescopic clarity the scene of a cow chewing by green indistinct waterbanks of a flooded field that the sky, having been fatally stabbed, had fallen into. A hedge unfurled behind the cow that stood forlorn as if it would be trapped should the water rise further — which it could not do under such moist sunshine.

Gone.

Railway trucks at station sidings fell back along the line like dominoes.

Gone.

An ochred farmhouse came, and stood for a second to show a grey slate roof, damp as if one big patch had settled all over it, the yard around flooded with mud and a man standing in it looking at the train. He waved. Ivan lifted his hand.

Gone.

A junction line vanished into the curve of a cutting.

Gone. All going or gone. They were still, who were gazing out of the windows, and everything was passing them.

The train found its way along, seemed to be making tracks as it went and leaving them brand-new behind, shining brightly when they turned a wide bend and Ivan stretched his neck to look back. An older boy smiled: 'Have you seen my new toy?'

He was sullen at being taken from such never-ending pictures that seemed to belong to him. 'No.'

'Do you want to?' He put an object on the table, ovoid, rubber, with four short legs as hands and arms. A length of fine tubing ran from its back to a hollow reservoir of air – which the boy held in his hand. Ivan stared at the rubber, in spite of not wanting to, then at the object on the table that sprang open and up, a horrific miniature skeleton, ready to grow enormously in size and grab everyone in sight, throttle them one and all and send them crushed and raw out of the window – starting with Ivan.

He drew back, and Stanley laughed at his shout of panic, hoping the boy would go on working it so that he too could enjoy the novelty. 'Stare at it like a man, then you won't be frightened! It's only a skeleton.'

When the boy held it to Ivan's face, it became the arms and legs of a threatening silver spider brushing his cheeks. Fields rattled by but gave no comfort, so closing his eyes he buried his head against his father. 'You are a silly lad. It's only a toy.'

'Make him stop it. I don't like it.' But he looked again at the glaring death-head, phosphorus on black, shaking and smiling, arms and legs going in and out as if in the grip of some cosmic agony. Amy came along the gangway at his cry and knocked the boy away, daring his near-by mother to object. She took Ivan on her knee: 'He was frightening him, you damned fool,' she said to Stanley. 'Couldn't you see?'

The train stopped at a small station. A gravel depot was heaped between two wooden walls, and beyond the lines a rusting plough grew into an elderberry bush. No one got on or off the train, which made the stop boring and inexplicable. People rustled among baskets and haversacks for sandwiches and flasks of drink.

'I want some water,' Ivan said, staring at the open door of the waiting room.

'You'll have to wait,' Amy said.

'There's an hour yet,' Stanley reminded her. 'He can't.'

The train jolted, as if about to start. 'I'm thirsty. I want a drink of water.'

'O my God,' his mother said. 'I told you we should have bought some lemonade at the station.'

'We had to get straight on. We were late.'

'A couple of minutes wouldn't have mattered.'

'I wanted to get seats.'

'We'd have found some somewhere.'

To argue about what was so irrevocably finished infuriated him, but he deliberately calmed himself and rooted in the basket for a blue plastic cup. His whole body was set happily for action: 'I'll just nip across to the tap.'

'The train's going to start,' she said. 'Sit down.'

'No, it won't.' But he didn't get up, paralysed by her objection.

'Are you going?' she said, 'or aren't you?' A vein jumped at the side of his forehead as he pushed along the crowded gangway, thinking that if he didn't reach the door and get free of her in a split second he would either go mad or fix his hands at her throat. Their carriage was beyond the platform, and he was out of sight for a moment. Then she saw him running between two trolleys into the men's lavatory as another playful whistle sounded from the engine.

'Where's Dad gone, Mam?'

'To get some water.'

Everyone was looking out of the window, interested in his race: 'He won't make it.'

'I'll lay a quid each way.'

'Don't be bleddy silly, he'll never get back in time. You can hear the wheels squeaking already. Feel that shuddering?'

'You're bleddy hopeful. We'll be here an hour yet.' The face disappeared behind a bottle: 'I'll live to see us move.'

Money was changing hands in fervid betting.

'He will.'

'He won't.'

At the second whistle he bobbed up, pale and smiling, a cup held high, water splashing over the brim.

'What's Dad out there for?' Ivan asked, lifting his face from a mug of lemonade someone had given him. The wheels moved more quickly, and Stanley was halfway along the platform. Odds were lengthening as he dropped from view, and pound notes were flying into the bookie's cap. A woman who wanted to place two bob each way was struggling purple-faced to get from the other end of the carriage. Her coins were passed over.

Amy sat tight-lipped, unwilling to join in common words of encouragement even if it meant never seeing him again. Their return tickets were in his wallet, as well as money and everything else that mattered, but she wouldn't speak. He can wander over the earth till he drops, she thought, though the vision of him sitting outside some charming rustic pub with twelve empty pint jars (and the plastic cup still full of water) in front of him, while she explained at the other end about their lost tickets and destitution, didn't make his disappearance too easy to keep calm about.

The carriage slid away, a definite move of steel rolling over steel beneath them all. He was trying not to spill his hard-won water. A roar of voices blasted along the windows as the train gathered speed. 'He's missed it!'

The door banged open, and a man who had slept through the betting spree jumped in his seat. He had come off nights at six that morning and his false teeth jerked so that only a reflex action with both hands held them in the general neighbourhood of his mouth. Red in the face, he slotted them properly in with everyone looking on.

'What's the hurry, you noisy bogger?' he asked, at Stanley standing upright and triumphant beside him.

They clamoured at the bookie to pay up, and when his baffled face promised to be slow in doing so they stopped laughing and threatened to throw him off the bleeding train. He'd seen and grabbed his chance of making a few quid on the excursion, but having mixed up his odds he now looked like being sorted out by the crowd.

'Leave him alone,' the winners shouted. But they clapped and cheered, and avoided a fight as the train swayed with speed between fields and spinnies. Stanley stood with the plastic cup two-thirds full, then made his way to Ivan and Amy, unable to understand what all the daft excitement was about.

'What did you have to make a laughing-stock of yourself like that for?' she wanted to know.

'He needed some water, didn't he?'

'You mean you had to put on a show for everybody.' Their argument went unnoticed in the general share-out. 'You can see how much he wanted water,' she said, pointing to his closed eyes and hung-down lower lip fixed in sleep.

The sea was nowhere to be seen. They stood on the front and looked for it. Shining sand stretched left and right, and all the way to the horizon, pools and small salt rivers flickered under the sun now breaking through. The immense sky intimidated them, made Skegness seem small at their spines. It looked as if the ocean went on forever round the world and came right back to their heels.

'This is a rum bloody do,' he said, setting Ivan down. 'I thought we'd take a boat out on it. What a place to build a seaside resort.'

She smiled. 'You know how it is. The tide'll be in this afternoon. Then I suppose you'll be complaining that all the sand's under water. It's better this way because he can dig and not fall in.'

A few people had been on the beach but now, on either side, hundreds advanced on to the sand, hair and dresses and white shirts moving against the wind, a shimmering film of blue and grey, red and yellow spreading from the funnel of the station avenue. Campstools and crates of beer staked each claim, and children started an immediate feverish digging as if to find buried toys before the tide came back.

'Can I have a big boat?' Ivan asked as they went closer to the pier and coastguard station. 'With a motor in it, and a lot of seats?'

'Where do you want to go?' Stanley asked.

Ivan wondered. 'A long way. That's where I want to go. A place like that. Up some road.'

'We'll get you a bus, then,' his father laughed.

'You want to stay at home with your mam,' she said. They walked further down the sand, between people who had already set out their camps. Neither spoke, or thought of stopping. Gulls came swooping low, their shadows sharp as if to slice open pools of water. 'How much more are we going to walk?'

'I didn't know you wanted to stop,' he said, stopping.

'I didn't know you wanted to come this far, or I wouldn't have come. You just walk on and on.'

'Why didn't you speak up, then?'

'I did. Why didn't you stop?'

'I'm not a mind-reader.'

'You don't have to be. You don't even think. Not about other people, anyway.'

'I wanted to get beyond all this crowd.'

'I suppose you wanted to dump us in the sea.'

'I didn't want to sit all day in a café like you did, and that's a fact.'

'You're like a kid, always wanting to be on your own.'

'You're too bossy, always wanting your own way.'

'It usually turns out to be better than yours. But you never know what you do want, anyway.'

He was struck dumb by this irrational leap-frogging argument from someone he blindly loved. He stood and looked at the great space of sand and sky, birds, and a slight moving white beard of foam appearing on the far edge of the sand where the sea lay fallow and sleepy.

'Well?' she demanded. 'Are we traipsing much further, or aren't we? I wish you'd make up your mind.'

He threw the basket down. 'Here's where we stay, you hasty-tempered bitch.'

'You can be on your own, then,' she said, 'because I'm going.'

He opened a newspaper, without even bothering to watch her go – which was what she'd throw at him when she came back. 'You didn't even watch me go!' He should have been standing up and keeping her retreating figure in sight – that was fast merging with the crowd – his face frowning and unhappy in wondering whether or not he had lost her for ever.

But, after so long, his reactions would not mesh into gear. They'd become a deadeningly smooth surface that struck no sparks any more. When she needed him to put an arm around her and tell her not to get excited – to calm down because he loved her very much – that was when his mouth became ashen and his eyes glazed into the general paralysis of his whole body. She needed him most at the precise moment when he needed her most, and so they retreated into their own damaged worlds to wait for the time when they again felt no need of each other, and they could then give freely all that was no longer wanted, but which was appreciated nevertheless.

'Where's Mam gone?' Ivan asked, half-hidden in his well-dug hole.

'To fetch us something.'

'What, though?'

'We'll see.'

'Will she get me a tractor?'

'You never know.'

'I want a red one.'

'Let's dig a moat,' Stanley said, taking the spade. 'We'll rig a castle in the middle.'

He looked up from time to time, at other people

coming to sit near by. An old man opened a camp-stool and took off his jacket. He wore a striped shirt over his long straight back, braces taut at the shoulders. Adjusting his trilby hat, he looked firmly and unblinking out to sea, so that Stanley paused in his work to see what he was fixing with such determination.

Nothing.

'Shall we make a tunnel, Dad?'

'All right, then, but it'll crumble.'

The thin white ray was coming towards them, feather-tips lifting from it, a few hundreds yards away and suddenly no longer straight, pushed forward a little in the centre, scarred by the out-jutting pier. It broke on the sand and went right back.

'She'll be in in a bit, don't worry. We're in the front line, so we'll have to move,' the old man said. 'Half an hour at the most. You can't stop it, and that's a fact. Comes in shoulder-high, faster than a racehorse sometimes, and then you've got to watch out, even from this distance, my guy you have. Might look a fair way and flat one minute, then it's marching in quick like the Guards. Saw a man dragged in once, big six-footer he was. His wife and kids just watched. Found 'im in the Wash a week later. Pulls you underfoot. Even I can find my legs and run at times like that, whether I'm eighty or not.'

If it weren't for the trace of white he'd hardly have known where sky ended and sand began, for the wetness of it under the line was light purple, a mellower shade of the midday lower horizon. The mark of white surf stopped them blending, a firm and quite definite dividing of earth and water and air.

'Come here every year, then?' Stanley asked.

'Most days,' the man said. 'Used to be a lifeboatman. I live here.' His hand ran around the inside of a straw basket like a weasel and pulled out a bottle of beer. He untwisted the tight cork, up-ended it, and swigged it into his bony throat. 'You from Notts, I suppose?'

Stanley nodded. 'I'm a waiter. Wangled some time off for a change. It don't make so much difference at a big hotel. There used to be a shortage, but we've got some of them Spanish chaps now.' His jacket and tie lay on the sand, one sleeve hidden by a fallen rampart of Ivan's intricate castle.

Looking up he saw Amy making her way between patchwork blankets of people, a tall and robust figure wearing a flowered dress. A tied ribbon set hair spreading towards her shoulders. She never tried to look fabricated and smart, even on her job as a cashier at the local dance hall. He was almost annoyed at being so happy to see her, yet finally gave in to his pleasure and watched her getting closer, while hoping she had now recovered from her fits of the morning. Perhaps the job she had was too much for her, but she liked to work, because it gave a feeling of independence, helped to keep that vitality and anger that held Stanley so firmly to her. It was no easy life, and because of the money she earned little time could be given to Ivan, though such continual work kept the family more stable than if as a triangle the three of them were too much with each other – which they wanted to be against their own and everyone's good.

She had sandwiches, fried fish, cakes, dandelion-and-burdock, beer. 'This is what we need to stop us feeling so rattled.'

He wondered why she had to say the wrong thing so soon after coming back. 'Who's rattled?'

'You were. I was as well, if you like. Let's eat this though. I'm starving.'

She opened the packets, and kept them in equal radius around her, passing food to them both. 'I didn't know how hungry I was,' Stanley said.

'If anything's wrong,' she said, 'it's usually that – or something else.' She reached out, and they pressed each other's hand.

'You look lovely today,' he said.

'I'm glad we came.'

'So am I. Maybe I'll get a job here.'

'It'd be seasonal,' she said. 'Wouldn't do for us.'

'That's true.'

While Ivan had his mouth full of food, some in his hand, and a reserve waiting in his lap, she asked if he wanted any more. Even at home, when only halfway through a plate, the same thing happened, and Stanley wondered whether she wanted to stuff, choke or stifle him – or just kill his appetite. He'd told her about it, but it made no difference.

After the meal Ivan took his bread and banana and played at the water's edge, where spume spread like silver shekels in the sun and ran around his plimsolls, then fell back or faded into the sand. He stood up, and when it tried to catch him he ran, laughing so loudly that his face turned as red as the salmon paste spread on the open rolls that his mother and father were still eating. The sea missed him by inches. The castle-tumulus of sand was mined and sapped by salt water until its crude formations became lopsided, a boat rotted by time and neglect. A sudden upsurge melted it like wax, and on the follow-up there was no trace. He watched it, wondering why it gave in so totally to such gentle pressure.

They had to move, and Amy picked up their belongings, unable to stop water running over the sleeve of Stanley's jacket. 'You see,' she chided, 'if you hadn't insisted on coming all this way down we wouldn't have needed to shift so early.'

He was sleepy and good-natured, for the food hadn't yet started to eat his liver. 'Everybody'll have to move. It goes right up to the road when it's full in.'

'Not for another twenty minutes. Look how far down we are. Trust us to be in the front line. That's the way you like it, though. If only we could do something right for a change, have a peaceful excursion without much going wrong.'

He thought so, too, and tried to smile as he stood up to help.

'If everything went perfectly right one day,' she said, 'you'd still have to do something and deliberately muck it up, I know you would.'

As he said afterwards – or would have said if the same course hadn't by then been followed yet again – one thing led to another, and before I could help myself ...

The fact was that the whole acreage of the remaining sand, peopled by much of Nottingham on its day's outing, was there for an audience, or would have been if any eyes had been trained on them, which they weren't particularly. But many of them couldn't help but be, after the first smack. In spite of the sea and the uprising wind, it could be heard, and the second was indeed listened for after her raging cry at the impact.

'You tried me,' he said, hopelessly baffled and above all immediately sorry. 'You try me all the time.' And the jerked-out words, and the overwhelming feeling of regret, made him hit her a third time, till he stood, arms hanging thinly at his side like the maimed branches of some blighted and thirsty tree that he wanted to disown but couldn't. They felt helpless, and too weak to be kept under sufficient control. He tried to get them safely into his pockets, but they wouldn't fit.

A red leaf-mark above her eye was slowly swelling. 'Keep away,' she cried, lifting her heavy handbag but unable to crash it against him. She sobbed. It was the first time he had hit her in public, and the voices calling that he should have less on it, and others wondering what funny stuff she had been up to to deserve it, already sounded above the steady railing of the nerve-racking sea. An over-forward wave sent a line of spray that saturated one of her feet. She ignored it, and turned to look for Ivan among the speckled colours of the crowd. Pinks and greys, blues and whites shifted across her eyes and showed nothing.

She turned to him: 'Where is he, then?'

He felt sullen and empty, as if he were the one who'd been hit. 'I don't know. I thought he was over there.'

'Where?'

'Just there. He was digging.'

'O my God, what if he's drowned?'

'Don't be so bloody silly,' he said, his face white, and thinner than she'd ever seen it. Bucket and spade lay by the basket between them. They looked into the sea, and then towards land, unable to find him from their mutual loathing and distress. They were closer than anyone else to the sea, and the old lifeboatman had gone. Everyone had moved during their argument, and the water now boiled and threw itself so threateningly that they had to pick up everything and run.

'What effect do you think all this arguing and fightin's going to have on him?' she demanded. He'd never thought about such outside problems, and considered she had only mentioned them now so as to get at him with the final weapon of mother-and-child, certainly not for Ivan's own and especial good. Yet he was not so sure. The horror of doubt came over him, opened raw wounds not only to himself but to the whole world for the first time as they walked towards the road and set out on a silent bitter search through the town.

For a long while Ivan sat on the steps of a church, the seventh step down from the doors, beating time with a broken stick as blocks of traffic sped by. He sang a song, dazed, enclosed, at peace. A seagull sat at his feet, and when he sneezed it flew away. He stayed at peace even after they found him, and went gladly on the train with them as if into the shambles. They seemed happily united in getting him back at last. The effort of the search had taken away all their guilt at having succumbed to such a pointless quarrel in front of him. He watched the fields, and heavy streams like long wavy mirrors that cows chewed at and clouds flowed over and ignored.

He sat on his father's knee, who held him as if he were a rather unusual but valuable tip a customer in the restaurant had left. Ivan felt nothing. The frozen soul, set in ancestry and childhood, fixed his eyes to look and see beyond them and the windows. The train wasn't moving after a while. He was sleeping a great distance away from it, detached, its jolting a permanent feature of life and the earth. He wanted to go on travelling forever, as if should he ever stop the sky would fall in. He dreamed that it had, and was about to black him out, so he woke up and clung to his father, asking when they would be back in Nottingham.

THE ROPE TRICK

WHILE making an efficient fire on which to roast sausages, on a rock bed built between carob and olive trees in Greece, one of the happy-go-lucky girls called June, who was nothing if not stoned and with it (and with me) said: 'I can see you've done your time in Sherwood Forest.'

'Listen,' I snapped, feeding brittle wood into the smoke. 'There are two ways you can do time in Sherwood Forest. One is in the army, and the other's in the sanatorium. I did mine in the sanatorium, but as a stoker not an invalid, which was after I came out of prison and met the girl of my life – if I remember.'

They laughed. Yes, it was very funny. We were all recovering from a strong dose of the pot, and lay in deadbeat poses eating at bread, and sausages burnt in pine and juniper branches. A hot wind came from up the grey wall of mountain as if someone were wafting it down through the asphodel for our especial benefit. We got to talking about love, and to my surprise none of them thought much of it – though we all had our birds, and the birds were there, and they didn't wear feathers, either. Neither did I believe in love – though I had an idea I was lying as usual.

'The sooner you lose all trace of love, the better,' I said. 'I can see that now, having never got her, yet realized that she was the love of my life and was bound to have some influence on it.'

June moved over to let me sit on the tree-trunk after

such a selfless stint by the fire. 'Love is the end,' said Michael, 'the end; so go to greet love as a friend!'

'And turn queer,' someone shouted, I forget who.

The blue sea puffed its spume tops along all the caves of the coast, fisherboats smacking down into it, and swooping along. 'I can never turn anything,' I said. 'But I'll try and tell you about her, if you'll pass me some more of that resinated fishwater that in these parts goes for wine.'

I didn't even know her name — no name, no photo and hardly a face, yet the memory bites at me so often that I think it must end up a good one. Either that, or it will rot my soul.

They looked at me, my travelling companions, friends of the fraternity that one bumped into on the Long Grand Tour. They listened as always, which was pleasant for me, because if you don't have anything to say how can anybody know you're alive? And if people aren't sure whether or not you're alive how can you be expected to know yourself?

I was lucky to have a few good pennies left in my pocket on that raw October morning, for it meant I still had one at least without a hole in it, which may have accounted for the fine and heady feeling as I walked down Mansfield Road. Stepping off the kerb I almost became good for nothing but a few black puddings as a petrol lorry flowed an inch from my foot, but even that shock didn't shake my tripes, and the flood-roar of swearing stopped in half a minute. Buns in a baker's window looked as if pelted with coal-specks and baked in canary-shit, so I thought I'd rather throw my remaining coppers on a cup of cold tea in a dirty cracked cup with lipstick round the edges, for the half-hour buckshee sitdown would be a break from the never-ending traipse over concrete and cobblestones looking for a job, a hard thing to find after a long stretch of the penthouse.

But at least I'd paid society for my crimes, which as you can imagine made me feel a lot better. You think it did? When you've stopped laughing, I'll go on. No matter how much quad you get you don't pay back anything. Some who thieve were born to make good, can't wait between snatching the loot and getting pulled in, but I'm not like that, didn't hand back a shilling of all I took in spite of my spell in the nick, for it was spent before they got me.

When the powdery rain eased off, a blade of sun leapt a row of pram and toy shops, as sharp and sudden as if God had whipped out a gold-plated flick-knife to prise open a door and break in. But the sun went back. He'd changed his mind because the shops weren't rich enough, being the sort that could go bankrupt any day. I pulled up my collar for the umpteenth time, the changeable weather lifting clouds high only to let them fall low again. If this sly and treacherous rain kept on peeing itself I'd sit in the library for a dose of reading, I said to myself.

Being still so close to clink I told the other half of me things it might have thought healthier to forget. I remembered a tall man inside, with black hair and a Roman conk whose brown eyes stared too much for his own good. Up to then I'd thought only blue eyes could stare so much, but his brown ones gazed as if a fire blazed between him and the world. Maybe he glimpsed something that could never be reached, even beyond the blue skies of outside. He was down for a seven-year stretch after manslaughtering a pal who'd knocked on with his wife, and he had a habit of pushing a scrap of paper into anyone's hand he passed close to. One day I happened to be going by on exercise and felt something pressed into my own. Despite the friendliness I wondered how much of a good thing it was, for if it had been a cigarette you had to be careful it wasn't a choirboy getting round you, for it was a common move of theirs.

Back in my cell I opened the postage-stamp of lavatory paper and read LENIN written in wavy capital letters. He's a brittle worm-eaten nut, I said, throwing it away. Yet I changed my mind, spent time looking till my fingers groped over it, then swallowed hard into my stomach and went back to reading Byron – which was all I was fit for in those not so far-off days.

One morning he threw a terrible fit in the grub hall, and smashed everything his hands could reach. He looked consumptive, thin, almost without muscle, yet I saw a match of strength I'd never seen before. But the screws battened the roaring bleeder down and humped him off to the loony bin.

So he was buried alive, and I was stomping the cobbles in my freedom, rooting for work to stop me starving. Not that you're at liberty the minute you set your snout beyond that iron gate. Being let loose after a thousand days was both fine and dangerous, a well-concealed trap in front of eyes and feet to trip me up and send me a header into some well-stocked shop or house, and so once more into the bullock-box. It's like recovering from a broken leg or pneumonia, when you need a few weeks' convalescence for fear of dropping back. So I trod softly for my own raw good, looking normal but stepping along that piece of taut rope, which is all right when it's on the ground and your head is solid, but after jail it's as though the line is six foot above the pavement and needs but one flick of an eyelid to send you arse over backwards. You may be lucky and pick yourself up from the right side of the rope-walk, but then again you might wake with a black eye in a cell at the copshop before you know where you are, supping a cup of scalding tea that one of the bastards had brought so's you'll look good in front of the magistrate next morning – all because an unexpected windfall made you slip on to the bad side.

Air and bridgestones shook by the station as a black muscle-bound express boned its way out towards Sheffield. Coiling rubbernecks of smoke and steam shot above the parapet to spar with the sky, and I wanted to be in one of those carriages with a ticket and ten quid padding my pocket, fixed on a seat with a bottle of ale by one paw and a filled fag-case in the other, looking out at fields and collieries and feeling good wearing a new suit got from somewhere, my eyes lit up with the vision of a sure-fire job.

The steamy tea-bar was full of drivers and conductors, hawkers, tarts, and angels of the dole, but nobody I knew, thank God, for I wasn't in any mood to moan about the weather and shake my head over the next war. They couldn't drop the Bomb soon enough for me, right there and then. I had no property to lose, caught sight of myself in the mirror, not looking good for much, because prison and long walks searching for work had kept me thin, my suit elbow-and-arse-patched, and prime King Edward spuds at the back of my socks, and a gap in one of my boot-toes big enough to compete with Larry Adler on the mouth organ. I never was a handsome brute, with a low forehead, thin face, and starvo eyes, and a change of fashion hadn't yet made me as prepossessing as I am now – with hair nearly on my shoulders.

I'd shaved that morning with a razor-blade sharpened on the inside of a jam-jar, but still looked as if I'd spent three years in jungle not jail, hunted by tigers, and enormous apes, swinging like an underdone Tarzan over streams and canyons with never a second's rest from chasing and being chased by devils inside and out. You can see what a man is by looking into his eyes, I thought, though I hope not everything he ever will be. I'd stared myself out while shaving, because the mirror in our kitchen was no bigger than a postage stamp ripped in half, which was why the safety razor cut me to ribbons. That's how you see anybody though, through smashed bits of mirror, and nobody can say which way and in how many pieces the mirror was going to break when it dropped and gave that seven years' bad luck. But through the pattern of such glittering scraps it's easy to tell whether a person is used to being knocked about by the world and has no option but to let it, or whether he's got something in his brain and stomach that makes him spin into action like an ant with bladder trouble against all the bible-backed pot-loathing bastards of the universe.

The café had once been smart, done up for old ladies and tory widows to sup tea in while waiting for buses to take them home to matchbox bungalows and yapping mole-dogs, but now the chairs were slashed and battered, a late-night hideaway for beats and riff-raff, and the wet floor was scraped from hob-nailed boots and specked with nub-ends.

A swish bint behind the counter with a soft white face and long hair asked what I wanted, and I would like to have told her the truth, though even so her heart seemed pleased when I answered: 'A cup of tea, duck.'

I must have been dug right into myself, because I'd sat next to a girl without knowing it. Not that I'd have shuffled on to a quiet corner and brooded alone if I had seen her, but I might have sparked an opening shot before sitting down. Giving the sly once-over with one eye, I watched my drink slooshing from a hundred-watt brass tea-tub with the other.

The maroon coat had padded shoulders and thick cuffs, and she must have been walking in the rain, because I could whiff the fresh wetness of autumn on stale cloth drifting through tea-fumes and fag-smoke, and saw where raindrops had dried on the nearest cheek to me. Her face was dark, going to sallow because of thinness, and would have had a better complexion with more meat on it.

I liked the dark hair she had, for it fell on her neck in ringlets, as if the wind had blown it around before she'd had time to think of drawing a comb through it. I couldn't see her full face, but enough at this cockeyed angle to sense that something was wrong.

I made up a story saying that maybe she'd lost either husband, parents or perhaps a baby, was in a bad way and didn't know what to do now she'd finished her cup of tea.

A hand reached up to her face, a movement that startled me as if before then I'd been looking at a person not quite alive. She stared at the sheer mirror that rose like an empty sea above a rocky shore of Woodbines and matches, and the only two faces looking back from it were hers and mine, me at her and she at nothing.

I pushed my hot and untouched cup of tea across to her. 'Are you all right, duck?'

'What are you staring at me for?' she demanded – in such a tone that I knew she wouldn't feel too good if I answered the same way.

'I like looking at people.'

'Pick somebody else, then.'

'I'm sorry. I've been seeing the same dead mugs year in and year out behind bars, and that's enough to drive even a sane man crazy. The government's had me worried and bullied blind, and I'm just about getting back into my heart.'

After such reason she became more sociable. 'I see what you mean. I've never been in one of those places, but I suppose it is strange to be loose again.' She spoke softly, yet jerked her words out in a breathless way.

'You catch on quick.' I pushed a fag over, one of a couple lifted from the old man's packet that morning before he pushed me into the yard and told me never to come back because the sight of me made mother ill. I took him at his word, and never did see either of them again.

She hesitated. 'I shouldn't smoke.'

I scraped a match along the brass rail. 'Don't take down, then it wain't hurt.'

'I haven't the price of a cigarette,' she said, 'to tell you the truth.' Hair and eyes made her sallow skin look darker than it was, and she could almost have been the sister of the bloke in clink who's plagued me with his Lenin message month after month. Smoking gave her more colour, coupled to the tea she sipped. 'I've neither digs nor a job at the moment. I was kicked out of both as from this morning.'

I lowered my fag, to get a clearer view of her face: 'What happened, then?'

'I worked as a wardmaid at the hospital.'

'I shouldn't think that'd be up to much.'

'It wasn't. I was scrubbing floors and serving meals from morning till night, and looking after dying men. It was a cancer ward. Did you ever see anyone die of that? Nothing kills the pain with some. They spin like crazy animals, right under the bed, and I had to help the nurses get them back and give them a jab.'

'It's the sort of work somebody's got to do.'

'I tried. But it wasn't possible.'

'Sure you did.'

'I went on all right for quite a long time, though I didn't enjoy it, but then I got ill and had to be looked after myself. Now I'm better, but I can't do that sort of work any more.' She wasn't the kind of girl I'd normally meet in the district I lived in, and maybe this as much as anything drew me to her. She wasn't so rare and extraordinary, but her nervous face hinted at more intelligence than usual, and I imagined that on happier days her slightly curved nose and thin lips would mark her as being witty and fond of a good time. She spoke in a clearer way than I did then, the headlights of that Nottingham accent dipped almost as if she came from some other town. I wondered how old she was, and thought she could easily have been thirty from the lines around her face. 'What part of the world do you come from?' I wanted to know.

She didn't like my question, but answered: 'Nottingham.'

I guessed she wanted me to mind my own business, yet went on: 'Why do you stay here, then, if you don't like it?'

'My husband.'

'He don't seem to look after you very well.'

'I've no idea where he is, and I don't much care.'

In spite of everything she seemed easier when I went on pumping her. 'Why did you split up?'

'He'd never work, expected me to go out and keep him. He's a wireless mechanic, quite clever, but I couldn't stand him any longer and left. Or he left me, rather. We had a room, and I had to leave that this morning because I couldn't pay the rent.'

The waitress was talking to a couple of postmen, so left us in the clear. I gave all the sympathy I'd got, for there wasn't much else I could part with, and feeling sorry for her made it seem less like trying to pick her up, for I wasn't sure whether I wanted to.

'That's the worst of working for these great institutions,' I said. 'They slave you to death then throw you out. They've got no heart. I know, because I was in one myself, with a big wall around it. They said my time was up, contract finished. I was a model worker and earned my remission, so I argued about the contract and rates of pay, said remission didn't worry me, yet told them that wages and conditions were rotten. But the boss swore at me, said he'd not take me on again when times were bad, that he'd let me starve if I didn't have less of my lip. I threatened him with a strike even, but before I knew where I was I was outside the gate, a hole in the arse of the suit I'd been taken in in.'

I looked at her through the mirror, and knew that nothing could dislodge the boulder of apathy across her brain and eyes. When people talk about apathy at election times they don't know what it means, I thought, hearing a speaker-van passing by outside asking us to vote for something or other.

Beyond her shoulders I saw rain falling, followed by hailstones in an October madness, a revolution of proletarian ice-heads rushing downwards to be softened by the still warm earth. A red bus came out of a rank, left gravel for tarmac and took a turning for Newark when the eyelids of the traffic lights lifted to a prolonged stare of green.

'I'd even like to be on that drowned rat of a bus going north along an up-and-down road,' I said, 'or rocketing down the motorway towards London.'

'Are you another who's always running away?'

People listened to the hail and rain as if the dim voice of God would start to come through it, so that her question couldn't be heard by anyone except me among the semi-darkness and clink of cups. 'I'm either running away from something,' I answered, 'or running into something, I don't know which. But I'm not a shirker, if that's what you mean.'

'Amen,' she said. 'Try running on nothing to eat, and no money.'

'You're right. I've done much on an empty stomach. That's why I've always landed in trouble.'

Tea and fags were finished, and she asked if I'd ever tried working. 'Many a time,' I said, feeling grim and rotten whenever I told the truth.

'I'm sorry. I'm sure you did. You seem wide awake enough.'

'Too pepped-up to find it easy. There's a shortage of work now: the bosses are frightened of losing their profits.'

She laughed — which in my stupidity I took as a good sign.

'My husband used to say that. I don't think it means much. Not that you're anything like him, though!' — remembering her previous opinion — 'Nobody could be as bad as he was, regarding work. He wouldn't go to bed at night and wouldn't get up in the morning. So we never had money, except what dole he wheedled, or National Assistance, or what I brought in. He didn't mind half starving, as long as he could sleep, and I think he'd really have been happy enough to see me on the streets.' This insistence upon work was grinding my nerves down, especially when I'd been wearing my legs off for the last fortnight trying to corner some.

She had no make-up on, not even lipstick, nothing to disguise the fact that she'd just fought clear of an illness. I wanted to get outside, but to leave her seemed too much of a risk. I glanced at her, not through the mirror but into flesh and blood, and, seeing her eyes closed felt afraid she'd faint, so put my arm behind her in case. Her mouth trembled, and tears came from beneath her eyelids, which gave me real distress, because in a way I liked her and felt sorry there was no useful help in me. I couldn't even offer my handkerchief, it was so black.

The girl behind the bar thought we were having a silent set-to, so stayed away and punched open the till as she served a customer, dropped a coin in with a dull click (which told me how full it was) and scooped out some change. Money. That's all she needed, a good meal, a few drinks and a warm bed, and she'd be a different woman. I pressed her hand till she looked at me. 'Wait half an hour, duck, and I'll have something for you, to help while you get a job.'

She nodded, unbelievingly. 'You wain't go away?' I said. She shook her head. 'Everything'll be all right when I come back.' She couldn't answer, was numb inside and out, and had no faith in what I was trying to say. 'You believe me, don't you? I won't be long. I know where I can get some money.'

I could have smashed my dum-dum head against a wall I felt so useless, but she nodded when I asked her again to wait just half an hour.

The rain had stopped. Nothing and no one – the sky least of all – has a mind of its own.

There were no pictures in the sky, so I looked at the gutters running with brown water, a full spate of production thrusting a straight way between kerb and cobblestones and leaving fresher air in its wake, dragged under further down by sewer grates and carried unwilling to the black and snaky Trent. Whether you fight with all the force in your spring-jack arms to make headway, or roll along like oil and water, you're sucked into the black grates of death just the same.

Thoughts come to me in grey and enclosed places, and in clink I closed my hand over and set them in the warm nest of my brain to stop me going into screaming madness. I remember the pals I had at school and see their lives, how they were mostly married by twenty-one, and an aeroplane flies out of heaven, sky-writing THE END across their world. Or they finish with the army and see the same message. But I was in the nick till twenty-four, and the army would never have me, so I'm still on the advance towards new fields and marshes. That two-word telegram can't frighten me, and when I came from the cell and under an archway the plane quickly wrote THE BEGINNING and flew away from the chaos that surrounds my life. Hemmed in with my shattered brain I sometimes saw myself as the man who, after hydrogen bombs have splattered the earth, will roar around the emptiness crying out word by word the first chapter of the Bible, because nothing else will be in my head except that, and whoever I meet won't have anything in their heads at all. Sometimes you go mad to stop yourself going mad.

Slab Square's dominating timepiece handed out twelve o'clock like charity. How could I get money for what's-her-name sitting in the tea bar? Print it, mould it, stamp it out like a bloody blacksmith? I zigzagged through the bus station and stood by the market watching people go in and out. She's expecting me back with something borrowed from a barrow-boy pal who happened to be conveniently near, and I thought: if only the world was made like that.

I walked between the stalls with weasel eye and

hungry hand set for any chance at all. Above the bustle of women buying supplies for their family fortresses, and old men looking at stuff they were too slow to pinch and too broke to buy I listened to cash-tills ringing in and out like the bells of Hell. Ping! Ping! Here, they were saying, here! Pinging like shots against a barricaded bank, while I stood spellbound in midstream of a strong crowd current, petrified with pleasure at the irregular rhythm and chorus of it, coupled with the call of voices, the clash of pots from crock stalls, breezes of fish and fruit and meat and the low thundering pass of traffic from outside. Money was pouring into pockets and tills, filling baskets and banks, hearts with greed and eyes with incurable blindness. Ping! Ping! And here was I with a poor bit of a rundown woman who was short of a few bob to stand on her feet, while a poster outside told me in dazzling colours I'd never had it so good and would soon have it better.

A sweet old Dolly-on-the-tub swayed by, a head-scarfed hot-slot from Notts with a homely mangel-wurzel face, a dyed army overcoat on her back. A purse lay in the basket between a packet of soapflakes and a wrapped loaf, so I followed the trail of her steamy breath. The place was jammed, and if my life had depended on a clear way through, all trouble would have been finished for good. Near the wide entrance my hand snaked and struck towards the basket, and in my imagination had already opened the purse, cursing my luck as I flung away bus tickets and pawn tags, pension book and worn-out photos, wading through all that to find only eighteen pence, because she'd never had it so good either. She swung towards the fish section, leaving my hand in mid-air and my bent back locked in a terrible lumbago cramp.

The fishmonger lapped paper around her bundle,

slapped it on top of the purse. A pal of Dolly's pulled her by the elbow, nearly crushing my toes. 'Can't abide this weather,' she said, after greetings. 'I just can't abide it, Mary, my duck.'

Mary couldn't, either, because it brought on her railway-husband's bronchitis. Such talk gave my hand the twitches, for it hovered like a semi-black meaty rare tropical butterfly near the back of my neck and was trying to get down between a butcher's assistant and a bus conductress, then through to the basket and purse that I couldn't even see any more. I had to look as if I were moving without really doing so, appearing cheerful and treadmill mobile as if on my way to the teastall whose cups steamed not far beyond.

'Aye, it does take some beating, don't it? I wouldn't mind it so much, except that I can never get my washing done, and it stokes my rheumatics up summat wicked.'

A deep sigh came from Mary, and I was close enough to blow in her ear, though still couldn't steer my mauler through. A couple of other women were jammed near. 'Well,' Mary grumbled, 'you mustn't grumble. You'll allus find somebody worse off than yourself.' You're looking right at him, I thought, unless I can get my hand on your pal's change-bag.

The way cleared, and I could see through to the basket, and when my hand was getting scratched on the straw I noticed the glassy eyes of the mackerel that had rolled from their paper specially to glare at me: 'You bring your thieving fingers any closer,' they seemed to say, 'and we'll scream.' Someone pushed, not heavy enough to be on purpose, but I was a few inches back again. He had difficulty getting through, and the roll of his fat neck came dead-level with me.

My heart crashed in and out like an oxygen bag, and

my feet moved from the cloth I was staring at, because I'd seen the colour of that uniform a good few times before: blue-black and ready for that stainless Sheffield flick-blade I'm glad I didn't have or, being so close to falling from the post-penthouse tight-rope I might have buried it between his shoulder-bones and run for my spent life. I made for the exit, the purse out of my mind, and hearing only the quick dying trail of someone swear as I put my foot on theirs without stopping to apologise.

I leaned against the wall outside, my heart and blood signalling far and wide the news of my miraculous escape. Then I remembered the girl in the café who was down on her luck and waiting for me to lope in, my sound pocket stuffed by the wherewithal to do her a lot of good. And in the same crashing breath I hated myself like arsenic because I'd thought of robbing a poor old trot of her short-changed purse, a woman worth ten of me because she'd suffered more and was older, while I hadn't and was still young. I could have smashed my head on a railing spoke and ended it all, because if I robbed anyone at all it shouldn't be anybody like her.

A bus drew in at the stop and people got off, stuffing used tickets like good citizens into the slot provided, being as afraid of dirtying the street as they were of shitting their own pants, wanting to keep the roads clean even though their hearts might be black. One four-eyed bowler-hat even put some coins into a little red box for uncollected fares. Luck puts the wind up some people. You've got to pay for everything in this life, old-fashioned church voices whisper from the insides of their hollow skulls, and so they believe it, young and old, clutching a conscience like an extra arm they can't do without, but which is really a rudder steering them through a life they've got used to and never want to change, since they're dead scared of anything new. And you can only change such a system by chopping that arm right off and burying it six feet under like any corpse. I was hungry and bitter, and knew it was wrong to be either, so told myself to stop it, stop it, or I wouldn't be free much longer.

I considered getting on a bus and opening one of those little red boxes, but threw the idea out because even though I might be a robbing bastard I was no fool. Walking towards Hockley I felt sure the girl would wait till I got back, for her present mood was familiar to me, had often nailed my body and soul into the ground and kept it there for countless hours so that I hardly knew time was passing and didn't care whether I died or not.

But now I was a man of action and wondered whether I should go to a bookshop and nick an expensive manual on engineering and sell it secondhand for ten bob or a quid. Useless. I turned from the clothes shops whose fronts were decorated with overalls, cheap suits, and rows of boots. I passed their prices labelled in big creosote figures, then walked between deserted lace factories and tall warehouses, booting a black rat-killing tomcat that ran from under a wooden gate. A few office tarts were strolling around, but I went through them like a ghost, and sat on a stone bench by a churchyard thinking that maybe I ought to go into Woolworth's and sneak my hand up like a cobra to drag down a few fountain pens.

Pacing the green old gravestones I came face to face with a church door, pushed it open and went in. There were rows of empty seats and a deserted altar, as if it were never used even by the rats. I read notices about this and that meeting, or service, or charity, and on a table lay booklets telling of church and parish history. But my eyes moved to a lightly padlocked box on which was painted in white letters: RESTORATION FUND.

I was outside in a second, but stopped for some reason on the steps. Feeling rain I had good reason to go back inside, but seeing granite scrolls and marble slabs, caskets with hangdog flowers, railings with heads like barbarian spears, emptiness crossing the narrow streets like an unhurrying copper, an exhausted sky only stopped from falling flat on its guts because of sharp chimneypots and pointed eaves, I had better reasons for staying where I was. Yet something put its hooks in me, and necessity like boiling oil burned away conscience and hesitation. I can't say I stood there reflecting like an honest man on good and evil, because it would be a lie if I did, but it was something to my credit that I stood there at all.

A few minutes later I pushed that oak-stained door once more and stood inside the church before it had time to slide to behind me. A piece of matting lay in front of the padlocked box, as if to encourage people with cold feet to step on it for long enough to part with their lolly, and I hoped it had been successful as I too stood and took a last glance around the church to make sure it was empty.

I looked at that lovely phrase saying RESTORATION FUND, which was the right one anyway, for I could think of two people at least who wanted restoring. Gripping the padlock as if about to do a clever judo move and sling the box skyhigh over my shoulder, I gave it a maniacal twist, my other hand pressed down hard on top. The wrench was strengthened by desperate need choking the girl I'd left in the café and it was plain, as the screws gave and the lock buckled, that a tenth of such force would have been sufficient.

I threw the lock on to the matting, and lifted the lid to see at least a pound in coin. It was strange how most of the money had dropped in and rolled to the left side of the box. I couldn't get a grip on the last few with my fingers, took some time getting fingernails under each before flicking them up into my hands where they rattled with a willing heart at freedom, glad like a bunch of prisoners at being in circulation again. An idea of gratitude struck me, of which I was always full, and because I rarely had the opportunity to give it I felt in my pocket for a pencil and wrote plainly under RESTORATION FUND: 'Thank you, dear friends.' I then dropped the cash pell-mell into my pocket and walked out.

People might think I've been in to light a candle for my grandmother's soul, and that I'm pleased she's being warmed at last in stone-cold heaven – I laughed as I went between gravestones into the street, then back towards the bus station café, where the girl no doubt sat looking into an empty teacup, unable to read her fortune because a leafless tea-urn had taken even that kick away.

Calmness left me. The older I was the more scared I got afterwards, not like the old days when I stashed open a post office in a light-hearted devil-may-care way and came out with a cashbox under my coat – and ran straight into the arms of a copper. The old lags had weighed me up right in saying I'd lose my nerve sooner or later. I used to think they were wrong and couldn't tell a cut lip from a black eye no matter how long they looked, but truth was somewhere at the back of it, because my legs would hardly hold as I turned by the market. With my rattling pocket I felt as if fifty sharp-cornered cashboxes hung around me like a Christmas tree at the wrong season. But losing your nerve doesn't matter so much, as long as you keep a tight control over yourself.

I was some way down from the bus station café where I'd left my dark and beautiful stranger, and being so close I dared at last to plunge my hand in and feel those cool shapes of money. A strong and wilful hand fell on my shoulder.

I'd have dropped stone dead on the spot if the life force hadn't thought I was worth saving at the last moment. Bleak terror sent me totally cold – before the voice broke. I was in court, given up as a bad job and put away this time for good, plunged into the cattle-pens of no-man's-land for what days were left to me, finished at the turn of a frost-filled iron key. My mouth was full of iodine and sawdust, coal gas and common bird-lime, and it stayed just as strong as ever when I heard the big bluff voice that followed the blow on my shoulder: 'You thought I was a copper, didn't you, you rogue! Still the same Jack Parker who can't keep his hands to hisself! I'd a known you a mile off, walking along like a hungry jack-rabbit.'

I turned, and who should it be but my old pal Terry Jackson, whom I hadn't seen for three years and wouldn't have known but for his face, for he was dressed like a millionaire in a charcoal-grey suit and striped shirt, a small knotted tie and spick-and-span shoes. He was smoking a long cigarette and looked so well turned out that labels should have been stuck on him saying 'Fragile' and 'This Side Up' and 'Don't Bend', which made him altogether different to the cross-eyed scruff in a shattered coat who'd gone with me into that warehouse. He was well fed, built on meat and solid salad, not so tall as I was, but his fair combed hair smelled of scent and his shaved chops of eau-de-cologne. He hadn't exactly a film star's features, but money had lifted his chin higher and given an extra sparkle to his eyes, seemed to have made sure that wherever he stepped in his tailor-made shoes everything would shift out of his way. Even the pimples had gone without trace, packed up their pus in a hurry and left.

'I'll bet you thought your number was up. I can just see both your pockets stuffed with fivers,' he laughed.

'I wish they was,' I said, glad to see him. 'How did you drop into all this wealth? And don't tell me you earned it as an errand boy.'

He grinned, spent another bash on my shoulder. I bashed him back. 'I ain't seen you for years,' he said. 'My old pal! I thought you'd signed on for twenty-one with the army, or killed yourself in some other way. And driving along in my new sports bus I see you. As if that could be anybody else but Jack Parker, I thought to myself! Where you bin, then?'

'All over. After a month sunning myself in the Isles of Greece I went to live in France. Worked there a couple of years. Had a marvellous time. Better than this dump.'

'Why did you come back then?'

'Got fed up. You know how it is. Which is your car?'

He pointed down the kerb, at an open sports with a girl in it. It was red and thin like a lobster, the sort you'd buy at the fish shop rather than a garage, looking as if it would crack in two if you sat on the middle of it.

'It can do a hundred in the shade,' Terry said. 'The other day on the road to Newark, you should have seen it, skimming along like a speed boat. I daren't look at the clock. It was smashing.' The girl waved to him, to hurry back and stop talking to that scruff. From a distance she looked a stunner, fair-haired and well dressed, little pink fingers drumming the side of the car, but not too hard in case she dented it or disturbed her C & A hat.

'Nice piece,' I said.

This made him happy. 'She ain't a piece. She's my wife. Married her a year ago. Her old man owns roundabouts and sideshows at the fair. Loaded with dough, and lets me help myself. Loves me like a son – which he never had. Come on the fairground next week and look us up. She's got an aunt who tells fortunes. It's a scream. Allus says I'll come to a bad end, but it's only because I can't stop laughing. She'll tell your fortune if you come.'

I took one of the fags he offered. 'If I've got time.'

Gold cigarette-lighter. 'Mek time. What are you doing these days?'

I'd nothing to hide. 'Looking for a job.'

'You ought to find a wife. Settle down. If you want a job I know a factory office you could do. Dough comes in from the bank on Thursday night for payday time. Need a drop of gelly though, that's all.'

I pulled him up: 'I've just been inside for three years and want to stay out for good now. Anyway I think my luck's changed as from an hour ago.' I said this to save him offering me a job on his roundabouts, because he'd be scared of me walking off with the week's takings of some coconut stall, and I'd be afraid of ending up on a spinning roundabout that got me nowhere. 'Still live in Denman Terrace?' he asked. 'We had some good times there, didn't we? A terrible crumb-dump. Has it been bombed yet, do you know?'

'Don't think so.'

'Let me know when it has. I'll have a double whisky on it.'

'I'm going back to London next week,' I said. 'Get a

job on a building site. Or work as a railway porter. You have better times down there.'

He was impressed. 'No kidding? I'd go with you, but' – nodding towards his piece of skirt – 'I'm hooked.' He couldn't take his eyes off her.

'What's she like then?' I asked.

'In bed?' Before I could stop him his grey eyes lit as if to burn through any she-cat: 'Boy, she's marvellous. I never get tired. When I come it's like Siberia. It goes on and on, and there's no end to it. I'm flying, man! Flying!'

'Introduce me. You've set me on.'

'Come to Goose Fair next week, then I will. Don't forget.'

'All right. Meanwhile lend's a quid or two. I'll pay it back when I see you there.' I said this in spite of myself, because up to that moment I'd preferred to steal rather than borrow.

Like a good friend, he pushed a couple of five-notes into my hand, and even laughed over it. 'Plenty more where that came from!'

We cracked each other a few more times on the shoulder, then I watched him drive off, his ringed fingers waving farewell like a king as he clipped the traffic lights.

My pocket bursting its seams with money I went back to find Floradora, who'd at least have a good few quid till she found work enough to stay on her feet. The time I'd seen her had set my mad brain going about her marvellous hair, and unhappy face that was good-looking if she'd ever escape from the uppers of her luck. I hoped I'd be able to know her better and though it might not come off, I thought, pushing open the door, it could be worth a bit more than my dead life to get in there and try. What with that, and bumping into Terry Jackson, I didn't give a sod for any job or body, saw the nick as a fading bad dream, and the rain now behind me washing out the past and what blame was latched to it, making the way clear for some future I was ever too blind to see.

The same wet smoke and tea smells, and the stink of beans-on-toast greeted me, but I'd never felt less hungry in my life, eyed the line of backs stuck on each seat over supped cups and nibbled plates, so many people in caps and coats, I couldn't immediately find the girl for whom my pocket jingled and rustled. Terry's long cigarette was still young, and flipping off the ash I walked between the tables but knew she couldn't be at any one of them. The search was casual, went to the more likely bar, and from head to head again looking for dark ringlets on one bent slightly forward.

I put off the truth as long as possible, unwilling to tell myself she wasn't there, had vanished, flipped-out with worries that a few quid and what care I could give might have fixed, gone also with her red lips and dark skin and agile thinness and all the madness and gaiety that lurks in a girl who can become buried by such lunatic unhappy weather. Still unable to believe it, I said to the waitress: 'Remember me, duck?'

She leaned all her softness forward: 'Who wouldn't?'

'What happened to the woman I was sitting with half an hour ago?'

There was a quick dark scuffle in her memory. 'Wore a maroon coat?'

I nodded.

'She went just after you left. I thought she'd gone to look for you.' Perhaps she saw my disappointment, but there was no use hiding it. What they can't see they sense, and think you less of a man for keeping it quiet under your coat. She asked me who she was, and I lied for the third time that day: 'My wife.'

I walked out of the café and back into the streaming rain to look for her, my good pocket full like my heart to bursting, weeping and cursing that she hadn't even waited the promised half-hour.

I'd find a job, but I'd never see her again. To look for both in the next few days was possible, but the search turned out to be hopeless. That's the way things are arranged, in this super and abundant world, which must go on turning, like a dead pig over the slow fire of my body and soul.

After three months in the sanatorium working as a stoker and doing my penance for the sick and healing, I looked again, but all I found was Terry Jackson. I took him up on the job he'd offered, and one day after a ragbag year of saving, during which time I was often tempted to rinse my fingers in the till but didn't, a year of all work and no expensive pleasures, I set out on a gang-hitch to ancient Greece, to the happy isles, the lotus hash-land where I'll stay forever, meaning for a long as I'm able to think back on what I am and have been. The sun is good and healing, the sausages here are real meat, the sky blue and the wind sometimes bitter, but my love has gone and will never come back.

We walked slowly up the stony track, zigzagging like donkeys after a hard day in the blinkers, between cork and carob and pine and olive, flashes of sea to keep us happy in the sweat and heat of the climb, taking an hour to reach the village where somebody's friend had promised us another night's doss on the stone floor of a washhouse.

'You're a long way from Nottingham and all that now,' Michael said. Not as far as you might think, I told him. I thought distances were small to all of us, and time had less meaning still. I'm right, they say. Life has no meaning after all, so long live life! That way we'll live forever, I say. It goes on like this ever upward path, my bright bird chips out from two loops below. I love you for that, I say, blowing a kiss that she doesn't see. My feet are free and my eyes are hot.

Down here in the olive grove I'm a great one for my stories, because what else is there except the gift of the gab, the talk, talk, talk, to stop the black sea rushing in? But all I've got left is enough LSD for half a trip, and hash for half a blow. My foot-fare home I've got, and as for June I think she'll make out, staying or leaving, unless I throw her off the Acropolis the day after tomorrow on our way through.

All the cash is spent, until I can peddle another selection of Turkish Delight, or Indian Rope that you can vanish up easily enough, or Persian chopped rug you can actually fly on. So in the meantime I'll bum around or starve, in the hands of pot, pot God, hash heaven, the acid bath of hell and all delight, on the straight but corrugated path that widens when it gets closer and closer and over the deep dip on the edge of the world. But I'll go over it thinking of my dark-haired beauty, thin-faced and maybe at death's door, the one I never got, so lost. And a man like me can't ask for more than that. If he does he suffers too much, and that sort of thing went out with the angels, didn't it?

ISAAC STARBUCK

'Why don't you go out?' was something Beatty never thought she'd need to say to anyone she married, especially Isaac Starbuck. The kids were in bed, the house quiet. The odd car cracked by, the shout of a youth calling some girl. Fire rattled its flames, a knife and fork eating up coal. 'You do nothing but stay in night after night.'

'I know. I want to read, and there's no other time to do it.'

'Ah, cowboy books. War books.' She'd taken to knitting again. 'Let's see if this pullover's too long.' He stood like some robust animal ready for the slaughter, full of weight and dignity with which to incriminate the unthinking actions of the world. 'Sit down then, ox.'

'There's nowhere to go,' he said, 'in any case.'

'That's only because you're content to sit here. You won't bother yourself. Why don't you go and see Tom?'

'And play Monopoly? He switches off the TV because he thinks it's bad manners to have it on when anybody calls, then gets out his bloody Monopoly set after he's asked how you and the kids are. I want to talk – about the world, about politics, but all Tom's interested in is selling houses and hotels! It's kids' stuff.'

'I just thought you wanted to go out.'

'When I do, you want me to stay in. Make up your mind. I come back from a union meeting and you look at me as if I've been knocking on with some fancy woman.'

'Only because it's so late. Don't think I'd care, though, if you did go with somebody else. I might even be glad to get rid of you.'

'I'll bet you would. You'd run down to a lawyer to get a maintenance order even before charging off with the kids to Tom's and Mary's.'

She held herself back: 'I might surprise you by doing something you never thought I'd do. Like having another chap of my own, ready to go off with.'

'And the kids?'

'Yes. With the kids. I know somebody who'd have them this minute. He'd run if I was as much as to snap my fingers.'

'Snap, then,' he said curtly, 'and see if I care.'

'I don't want to. I'm just telling you.'

'Well, don't. I don't want to know.' Not that he was afraid for her, but he was scared for himself, any minute ready to go out on the wild. Such open talk made it seem as if they'd already done it on each other.

'You brought it up,' she said, 'talking about fancy women. I can see the way your mind's running.'

'Why don't you let it drop? I might have brought it up, but you're worrying it to death.'

'Still, don't let me hear of you with any woman.'

'You won't,' he said, shaken that they should talk about what had been dominating his mind for months.

'Not that I wouldn't know,' she taunted. 'You'd never be able to hide anything like that from me. I'd know in a flash.'

'There'll never be anything to know,' he said. 'Don't think I wouldn't be able to keep it from you, though, if there was. I wasn't born yesterday. Nor the day before yesterday, either.'

'You seem bloody sure of yourself.'

'You wouldn't think I was up to much if I wasn't, would you?'

'Not in that way, you deceitful rat. Don't think I don't keep an eye on you. We've got three kids, and they aren't going to suffer.'

He laughed. 'You've been reading too much of that *Woman's Realm* tripe. Nothing's happened, you know.'

'Maybe not, but watch as it don't.'

'Are you trying to tell me what to do and what not to do? Because if you are, you can pack it in. All you're doing is putting ideas into my head.'

'I can't put anything in as wasn't there before.'

'Don't be so sure. I'm as innocent as driven snow. I'm not guilty. All I've got suspicious is a few black-heads on my face, and that ain't through VD, either. If you can tell me when I might have time to carry on with other women I'd be grateful, because I can't think of any.'

After supper, she said: 'So you want to go on the loose? As if I didn't know. Men are all alike. They get married, make sure their wives have a house full of kids, then get out and enjoy themselves.'

'I think you want me to go on the loose,' he said, feeling lighter in mood with food inside him, 'the way you're talking.'

'I'm just trying to find out which way your mind lies.'

'Now you know.'

'Yes, now I know.'

'I'd rather do that than play Monopoly with that pop-eyed brother-in-law of yours, and that's a fact.'

'He's not pop-eyed. He's got more intelligence and

go in him than you'll ever have. At least he went to Canada.'

'He came back as well. It didn't get him very far.'

'Why don't you try it and see how far it gets you? You've got a few hundred in the bank.'

'That's to buy a car with. I've got my work here. When I've got no work, that's the time to get out. I don't like snow, so if I go anywhere it'll be Australia. Plenty of sun would suit me better.'

He bought a car the following spring. While lukewarm sun still lay over water and fields he'd take them at weekends and after work on long excursions up Trent valley, beyond Bleasby and Thurgarton, Farndon and Newark. Nothing more was said about him staying late at union meetings. Now it was: 'Why don't you ever take me out? You never take me.'

'That's a lie.'

'Calling me a liar now. I'm not a liar. I wish I was. As good a liar as you are, anyway.'

'I often take you out in the car, you know I do.'

'Always with the kids. A quick run ten miles out to Matlock or Southwell, a quick pint and then back. I mean out.'

'You want to go to Buckingham Palace and have tea? I'll get queenie on the blower. We go out on Saturday night, I could get you to the union meetings, but you aren't interested. You've met my pals, and you don't like them because we talk about work or politics. What more can I do?'

'I want some life,' she said.

'Why don't you go out on your own then? Or with Mary, or some pals? I won't mind.'

'I know you wouldn't. You'd just use it as an excuse to go off gallivanting.'

'You said you weren't jealous. Make up your mind.'

'I'm not jealous. It's just that I don't want you going all over the place.'

'I've got my own life. I'm not tied to your apron-strings.'

'And I've got my life as well.'

'Use it then.'

'I will. I'm not tied to your bloody boot-laces, either.'

'I wouldn't want you to be.'

'That's the trouble. You don't want me around at all. I think you'd feel fine if me and the kids vanished off the face of the earth. Then you'd be as free as you've always wanted to be.' The words stung, because she was dead right. But if he didn't swear blind she was dead wrong the marriage would collapse like dust and ashes.

11

Before he knew what was happening he'd fetched her a drink, and under the foggy noise of the pub was saying how much he loved her. She was slim, though well-figured, with a round face and short dark hair. Plump pale cheeks and a small mouth indicated a lascivious discontent. 'You've only just met me,' she said, 'so how can you know?'

'Because I could pick you up and carry you upstairs,' he said. 'If I was to try.'

'I don't weigh all that much, so it wouldn't make you a Samson.'

He drank: 'I never take a woman to bed I can't pick up. Golden rule. Have another.'

'No thanks. What's wrong with women you can't lift up?'

'Too fat. Half a pound of meat before you get to it. Your sort's more passionate.'

'I save my passion for my husband.'

'All married women should be like you.'

'Isn't your wife like me – like that?'

'I'm not married. Made up my mind at ten to stay with my mother all my life.'

'You've got too many answers. I don't trust you. I never trust a man who won't go to bed with a woman he can't pick up.'

Up in the bedroom she asked: 'Shall I take all my clothes off?'

'Of course,' he answered. 'You think I'm a pervert?' He was surprised at himself, one minute because he should have done it sooner, and the next because he'd done it already. Five years faithful to one wife must be a record. He was drunk, but that was no excuse. 'Where's your husband?'

'Away till tomorrow night.'

'Suits me,' – and he was in.

'Don't spill your cocoa,' and he wondered how common you could get.

His large grey car rumbled down the cobblestoned street, feathers of blue smoke spinning from its exhaust. The road was humping under him, a panel-beater's spoon thumping the gasometer top. Hanging between the rear fender and the last rib of the luggage-rack a man outside was fisting with all his might at the roof.

Isaac lifted his foot from the gas pedal, hoping his passenger would drop off without a twisted ankle or a blue-black face. Noise at work had been robbing him of sleep, the rattling brainkill of assembling tractors. Friday gave way to human noise, but now the insane drumming above his hungover tongue persisted all down the street. He slid his vehicle neatly to the kerb and, hating fuss and violence, got out and walked leisurely towards the back.

They collided with a shout, like two shields, but without damage. A morning paperboy heard the elder man say: 'I caught you red-handed, you foul rotter.'

Isaac denied nothing: 'Are you going to stop climbing on my car?'

'You filthy beast, with my wife.'

'Yes or no?'

'I want your name and address. This'll come up in court.'

'I know. But don't hit the roof of my car again like that, because I can't stand it. My whole system rebels against it at this time of the morning.' There was no answer. Face and hard words matched. A combined smack-and-knuckle snapped along the street.

He left the man dazed and muttering. Taking a corner with one hand, he flung out his broken unlit cigarette. The car glistened in weekend sunshine, metal and gentle heat mutually caressing, a well-polished wonderbug going between factory and railway yards. His left cheek was emery-papered from the scuffle. How was he to know the husband would be back so soon? But his wife should have, unless she liked seeing him get knocked about every week. Maybe he'll come around the pubs and pick me out when Beatty's there. I'll get that luggage-rack tightened in case he pulled it loose.

He didn't want to go home to his wife on this Saturday morning, nor kids – those brass-fisted tow-headed devil's anchors. Terry had fallen arse over backwards out of the bedroom window, somersaulting on to up-and-coming fungus while Beatty was in the kitchen frying his meat-slab for tea. A voice wailed above sizzling fat, and Terry was back on his feet before she could get to him, knees grazed into purple patches, yelling at the shock of seeing soil one minute and speeding along the plumb-line of his own stare the next. Meanwhile the pan was flaring and Isaac's burnt offering was too black to offer.

Alert and alive, he levelled the car-snout at Lenton steeple, wheeled right over the bridge, half-whistled music for the thinking stage spreading behind his brain – before which the audience of himself would laugh or jeer, so that a red-haired cyclist in shorts thought he was mocking her, and a pink tongue flashed in his mirror.

He turned north into the patchwork country. A rabbit-hutch bungalow stood for sale in a rabbit-food field. He imagined it worth three thousand pounds. Could get it for a couple of quid after the four-minute warning. Five bob, perhaps, as the owner runs terrified for the woods, hair greying at every step – if I wanted to own property and get a better deal in heaven.

Needle shivering at cold eighty, he felt something like love for the machine under him, the smooth engine swilled and kissed by oil, purring with fuel, cooled by the best water. Out of the rut of family, the trough of drink and the sud-skies of low-roofed factories, he flicked on his yellow winkers, pipped his hooter, and swung to overtake a vast lorry laden with castings and grinding Newarkwards – lips in a half whistle, mind emptiest at greatest speeds.

Going through London once he'd pulled up in a long line of Hyde Park traffic, dozens of cars on either side. When amber glowed he was across before others moved, laughing on his way to Victoria and down Vauxhall Bridge Road. But the other side of the river, he was confused by roundabouts and one-way streets until, exhausted and raging, he got his bearings by New Cross and went as fast as the now enveloping rush-hour allowed towards the nightdrenched hop-gardens of Kent.

Sweat ran down his face, and he put up his hand as if to brush off a fly. The needle seemed pinned at ninety, his eyes looking too hard at the road-belt unwinding under his wheels, flagged by signposts and a corridor of upright trees snowing off leaves in early sunlit autumn, everything fresh as a kid's crayon-drawing he might have done at school when jolted by the shock of something new. He couldn't look at his dial, but the odour of tarmac burning his tyres acted like smelling salts and drew his well-shod foot back from the pedal. Within a minute the speed was down to an anchor-dragging sixty and back on the right side of death, so that he could light a cigarette.

The pickings of freedom felt good, gave him a weight not known since before getting married, dream years ago. He'd had enough, had realized it for a long time but somehow had been frozen, stiff with indecision. Last night he'd broken free, but for how long? He was surprised that guilt had vanished so soon, in which case it may be possible to have a fling every so often, his marriage and Beatty being none the worse for it – though telling her where he'd been would need a few choice lies she'd never believe. What the eye doesn't see the heart doesn't grieve. That, anyway, would be better than a bloody rupture with tears and shrapnel spitting far and wide, and him in the middle burning to hell for something he couldn't now wear the credit for. Yet even that wasn't real trouble, could be solved and smoothed over if he wanted it to be.

Drawing down the windows, he felt cold air swording through the car as if frontier soldiers were stabbing hay-bales for escaping citizens. In spite of the blue sky, he shut it again.

III

'If you don't stop it,' she shouted at Chris and Terry fighting in their room across the landing, 'I'll come in and bang your heads together.' She sat at the dressing-table in her pyjamas, wondering where the hell Isaac was. 'Beatty Stathern, he'll never be any good to you,' my mother always said. But my mother was wrong, or had been until last night, for what else could you do but think the worst when Isaac-rotten-Starbuck was involved? Yet if anything was wrong with being out all night why wasn't she sobbing in some police station and pushing aside a mug of sweet tea some fatherly copper handed her?

He might be flattened under that fast car she'd tried all her might to stop him buying. He'd had no time for her since then, saved up year by year and after weeks of dog fight had settled for the car instead of a down payment on some bungalow at Cossal or Bramcote. As it was, he preferred to go on living in this hundred-year slum, and they would have been in two rooms still if Mam hadn't let us take it over when she died.

Luckily he never knew Mam's real opinion of him, otherwise he'd have called her blind. She was wrong though, because as far as I know, and I know it to be the truth, he ain't yet done it on me with a living soul, not in all the five years we've been married, and there's not many as hold out so long in this neighbourhood. I love him, and he loves me, but all the same, I'd love to know what he was up to last night.

Went to see one of his mates, I suppose, and his car broke down. He could have walked, or come home in a taxi. Perhaps he went to his sister's, took her for a drink and got too blindoe to drive back. I hate him boozing like that, tell him to do what it says on TV and stay sober at the wheel: 'There's two things I don't like when I'm kay-lied, and one is driving a car,' he said, a maddening smile all over his clock.

The bedroom suite was shabbier than when they bought it, plywood and paint-knocked, no gloss left on its hundred-pound exterior. But there wasn't much hope of getting a new one with that car costing the earth to run. The mirror signalled her face, hazel eyes of a cat in springtime, more magical (and in colour) than any television set, but disappointing because it cost less. Beatty's skin was clear and firm of a morning, matching her eyes and setting off the falling bands of auburn hair. Her head was delicately shaped, a fine forehead, ears with almost no lobes, lips sardonic and lively. Her unsupported breasts, round and firm under her tops, were clamped a little higher when she stood to dress. He doesn't know what he's missing, she thought. They say men wear better than women, but she had all her teeth still, whereas Isaac already had two false ones.

The kids were bumping the telly to bring on pictures – though she'd often told them it was too early in the day. Isaac once joked that the best time was at four in the morning, when they had an hour of blue movies. Hardly anyone knew of this, but he'd discovered it by accident on staying up all night when she was having Chris. He'd told her about it in such detail that she'd come even before they fell on to the settee.

She forced them to the table. 'Stay there and get your breakfast.' The first cup of tea was broached, drunk scalding by the odour of toasted bread. A heaped-up plate was brought in, and Chris snatched one before touchdown. She smacked his hand: 'Hold back, or you'll get my fist.' He pretended to cry, then splayed into laughter at the mock-docility of his brother. 'If you don't behave I'll tell your dad.'

She might, but where was he? They're the last bloody kids I'll have, I know that much, up to my neck in breakfast and house, while he's running around with some woman for all I know, unless he's in hospital covered in plaster of paris or laid out smashed to bits in a deadhouse. That would be the end of it right enough. A widow at twenty-six, though I've no fear that plenty would have me still.

The thought frightened her, a slice of toast going cold while dwelling on it. Dead houses and television sets, cars rumbling through outside sunshine, people calling to each other before Saturday shopping, didn't connect till such moments as this – as they had for tragic certainty when her mother died and Isaac was the one to soften it and do everything. My God! Whatever would I do if he's gone the same way? If he stepped through that door I'd throw this pot of scalding tea in his face, frightening me like this.

She went out of the back gate and turned towards the main road. At least the sun's out, though it'll still be cloudy for him when he gets back. Not that I care whether he does or not, since no excuse will satisfy me, because I've had my fill of him this last year or two. If he hadn't given me the housekeeping money before sliding off last night I'd have told Mary to put me up till I found a place of my own. And if I don't do that, it's only because there's no need and not because I don't want to.

At the butcher's she bought a fine-looking piece of lamb she knew he'd get stuck into after his walk and couple of pints on Sunday. He was healthy and in the spice of life, while some of those he'd gone to school with looked worn and balding in a way he never would, even at ninety.

By the bus stop she met her brother-in-law – thin, pale, long-jawed Tom. Nine-tenths of the time his eyes were rabbit-dead, as if he'd lost his job while others got a raise, buried his mother on August Bank Holiday, or just found his correct treble chance unposted while reading of someone else getting the two hundred thousand. But at Sunday tea he'd have the salad shaking with the rest of them by acting out those three conditions of his lost and gloomy face recalled by Beatty as they greeted each other at the fishmonger's.

With Mary and three kids he'd set off once for a new life in Canada. 'They need skilled carpenters like me,' he'd said. Eighteen months later he was back, docked at Liverpool one wet midsummer day. Isaac and Beatty met him, and coming over the pungent rainsoaked Pennines heard him preferring death to idleness, dishonour to destitution. Enveloped in the lugubrious sad pride of a man with no guts, he understood a lack of work in winter, but unemployment had for some reason lasted into summer, and Mary's confinement used up his savings.

A smart wind flicked the supermarket doors. 'What's wrong?'

She laughed: 'I'm worried about whether I'll make ends meet; I'm worried about whether my kids are all right in the house; I'm worried about whether Isaac will go on short time next week.'

'That's not worry, duck. That's life. What is it?'

'Isaac went out last night and isn't back yet. I'm wondering if anything's happened.'

He lit two cigarettes, gave her one. She recalled his words: If I hadn't met your sister I'd have married you, Beatty. I'll never forgive Isaac for meeting you first. 'I shouldn't worry about him. He can drive that machine like a pair of skates. And Isaac's not the sort to go on the tiles.'

'There's always a first time,' she said.

Maybe it isn't even the first time, he thought, though there'd never have been anything like that with me. 'Not with him. He'll be back. Perhaps the car broke down. Or he fell in with a crowd of pals from work. You know what they are. They wouldn't want to haul him back to you on a shutter, flat-out and groaning. They're considerate that way. Probably slept in somebody's parlour with a Co-op rug over him.'

'It's not funny. I'm worried to death. It's the first time he's done anything like this. Still, I expect he'll be back by dinnertime.'

'If he ain't,' he said, picking up her bags, 'I'll go and scout for him. I know a few of his haunts.'

IV

Ignition off, he surveyed the outside world, for the first time feeling unreal in his car, as if its walls barred him from the way of all true senses. He'd looked on it as his friend, horse, brother-in-arms, cockpit in which to speed through streets that deadened around him.

He walked fifty yards, then turned back because he'd left his lighter behind – unwilling to see anyone sent to jail or borstal for helping themselves to it. A policeman stood by: 'Excuse me, is this car yours?'

Isaac took his time locking the door. 'It is – if you want to know.'

'Well, I was asking you.'

'Well, I'm telling you.'

'What's your name?'

'Isaac. Starbuck.'

'Oh?'

'That's right.' Isaac saw through him, a pool of water, frogs-spawn and dead leaves, back to schooldays when some new bully had pushed him against a wall, demanding to know who had killed Jesus Christ because his name was Isaac. 'I did,' Isaac said, a savage bash into the middle of next week.

'Do you mind showing me your papers?' He was of similar build, more blue-eyed and less clean-shaven, a smile flickering further behind his eyes than in the ironic gaze Isaac turned on him. He lit a cigarette: 'What are you booking me on?'

'Don't get funny. I'm not booking you, I'm asking you for your means of identity.'

'You think this car isn't mine? Or that I've been nicking things from it?'

'I'd like to see your papers, or I'll have you down at the station.' What a story: phone Beatty, when they turned me loose from the cop-shop hoping to see the last of me before they burst into tears at the certainty of my suing them, and say look where I've been while you and Tom sat calling me blind for knocking-on with all the squidge tarts in Sneinton. 'Let's go then. My car will be safe enough for an hour or two now I've locked it.'

'I'm here to protect it,' the policeman said. 'I've watched you going to and from this car, and I haven't seen proof that it's yours yet. My job is to make sure nobody takes things from cars.'

'You should come and see my job,' Isaac said, also affable. 'There's no comparison.' If I'd had that worried-about-money look between my brows he wouldn't have bothered me. They stood like two brothers, one in plain clothes come to see what the other one wanted for supper that night. 'People slip me dough in my job,' Isaac said, 'and I don't worry 'em. Hear all, see all, and say nowt. The world couldn't get on without a bit of grease on the old palm. A town like this would fall to pieces. No transport, telephones, newspapers, shops, factories – everything dead. People on the streets rioting. All because of no bribes, no tips. How do you think I got my car? Honest work? Don't kid yourself. A commissionaire at our place died the other week, been on the gate twenty years. You know what he left in his will? It was in the paper. Eight thousand pounds. Eight thousand. On eleven pounds a week and five kids to keep? Tell me another one! My barber has an Austin Healey, and he didn't get that at three bob a nob either. Does a roaring trade in little girls and has a lezzie brothel in his bungalow at Wollaton. He said to me: "Isaac, you don't blame me, do you? I see all these nice cars floating about, so I want to have one. That's natural ain't it? I want twenty-two carat gold-tipped shoelaces, not to mention plutonium spec-frames. Everybody's got these things nowadays. I take my fancy-friends to Formentor instead of Blackpool." The world's got to go around,' tapping his car, 'and if I could think of a better way I'd cut my throat for being a dirty Red. Every man for himself in this marvellous world, because nobody can deny it's a terrific place, the way the money changes hands and blokes like us get jack-all for it.'

The policeman was amused: 'I was trying to see that your car was OK.'

'I appreciate it,' Isaac said. 'I'm off for a drink with my mates, so if you'd keep your eyes on it, I shan't forget you when I get back.'

'That's all right,' the copper said.

He'll expect a couple of quid, Isaac thought, but I'll steal my own car from under his snooping nose.

*

v

Pushing into the midday beerstink he spotted Freddy and Larry about to draw on their first full pints of the day. He felt himself back again in an all-enclosing world that he seemed to have been born and brought up in. Outside he'd not noticed the sun, but seeing it pour through the top windows made him feel more exalted than if he'd been in one of those churches he'd heard about.

'You're looking black today,' Freddy said. 'Have your kidneys burst or something?'

'I was out all night,' Isaac told them, unbuttoning his coat. 'My sister's husband's brother-in-law just got married, and I was heaved into his slosh-up after a joke at the registry office. I only meant to have a cup of beef-tea at my sister's, and was all set to leave at eleven but somebody said: "One for the road, just a small one" and then I woke up *on* the road, dog-ends and horse-shit all around me and a double-decker Trent Valley traction bus burning my headache off with its headlights and about to grind over me. So somebody carried me into his house, and I woke up this morning to the smell of frying bacon, and while this bloke was setting out the Pinocchio cornflake dishes I went into the next room, jumped his wife before she could say: "Hey what the bloody hell do you think you're on with?" then staggered downstairs to borrow her husband's razor for a shave. So you can imagine how I feel.'

'What a life,' Freddy said, 'it's full of sin. If I was out all night, even innocently, my wife would finish with me.'

'So would mine,' Isaac said. 'I want to ask you a favour. Will it be all right if I tell Beatty that I got too drunk to drive home, and that I made for your place? She'll believe you if you say I kipped there. You can back it up when you call for me next week on your way to the meeting. OK.'

One of the men at work said that Freddy was such a quiet sort that Bibles wouldn't melt in his mouth. Middling in height, he had high cheek-bones and was dark in colour as opposed to Isaac's yellowish robustness and Larry's texture of salmon pink. He was the oldest of the three, a studious-looking Jamaican who had been an air-gunner in the war and flown over Germany sixty times to see that his plane kept clear of fighters while flobbing down its four-tonners, belligerence which he now devoutly regretted. 'I've never told a lie in my life before,' he said with sincerity. 'You're the best pal I have, but I don't think I can do it.'

'Forget it then,' Isaac said. 'Come on, let me get you another, you boozing Baptist. I've had such a run-around last night that I'm ready to pour a barrel into myself. When I left that house this morning the husband was hanging on the luggage-rack of my car, so I had to stop and punch him off it. He just wouldn't let go.'

Freddy shook his head: 'You always seemed so steady to me.'

'Maybe. But I fell for that bint like a ton of bricks, and I wasn't even drunk. It was marvellous while it lasted. Let's drink to it.'

'I'm sorry it happened though,' Freddy said, drinking.

'The first time since I was married. And the last. I'm going home after this one. Not that I want to go home. I don't want to go at all. I'm knackered and brain-bashed, heartsore and full of stones. I want to walk across Africa, America, Russia. I've got more strength than I've ever had – but it's as much as I can do to lift this pint to my gob.'

'If you feel like walking,' Freddy said, 'walk. Can't you do what you feel like?'

Isaac lit a fag: 'It's got to come over you like a storm, so that you don't think at all, but before you know what's happening you're doing it.'

'You work enough. Do you want a war, or something?'

'If I knew what I wanted I wouldn't be chinning over a pint at Saturday dinnertime. And you stand need to talk about war, after your record. I'm glad you did it though, Freddy. If you hadn't they'd have had us in them death camps before we could pick up bricks to smash their heads in. I'm a Red, and not only are you a Red, but you're coloured as well. Fancy being born the way we are.'

'I'm not a Red,' Freddy corrected him. 'I'm a Baptist. I go to church, pray and study my Bible.'

'I don't know why I bother to talk to you,' Isaac said. 'If I was a Baptist I wouldn't know where to put my face.'

'If I was a Red,' Freddy answered, 'I'd get on my knees and pray.'

'Red's don't pray,' Isaac said. 'That's why I'm a Red.'

'Nothing's sacred to you,' Freddy told him.

'I know,' Isaac said. 'But don't worry: I shan't bring up your criminal past again. I don't see why you should be ashamed of bombing Germany, even though you was only bombing fellow-workers like us. You weren't to know. You was young in those days, immature. Don't get upset, Freddy. It was a tragedy, that's all.'

'Isaac, you're a bastard. Why don't you drop dead?'

'I can't. There's still some ale left in my jar. Come on, drink up. It wasn't true about bombing the Reds. I just made that up to get your goat. I'm the guilty one, because I was on to my mate the other day in the air force. He's an air vice-marshal. I got him on the phone: "Hello? RAF? Put me through to Jack. Jack? Isaac here. Look, do you think you could manage a thousand for tomorrow night? Sure, Germany. Nazis keep on coming up. Make a start at Düsseldorf, OK? Thousand off at seven. You can? You'd do anything for an old pal? Ah, I know you would, you dirty old man. Fine. I'll treat you to a pint when I see you. Any time. Missis? She's fine. How's yours? That makes eight, don't it? You'll have a football team in a year or two! Yes. Play each other. So long then." I know I'm a murderer, Freddy, for thinking things like that. My mind's full of evil thoughts, but so's everybody's.'

'What hope is there for mankind?' Freddy said. 'All I can do is pray for you.'

'That won't do me any good. You remember that Pole at work, Ted his name was, who got ten years for burying an axe in his mate's skull when they were pally and drunk? He told me one tea-break how he saw Germans in Poland making Jews dig their own graves. Then the Germans shot them all. I asked: "What did you do about it?" "Nothing," he said, "I just stood around". "I should have done something," I told him. Then a week later he kills his mate, full of friendship. What a world. That's why I got old Jack on the blower.'

'All I can do is pray for you.'

'You think I'm a sinner,' Isaac said, 'but you should have seen me before I was married. I didn't stand in pubs and talk. I used to get hold of all the women I could. A home-wrecker, I was.'

'It's terrible. But why did you get married then, and expose yourself to similar dangers?'

'I walked into a trap. All the time I was scattering my load some sly little bastard hiding in my liver kept saying: "Where's that trap? I've got to find that trap. I'll die if I don't find that trap, even if it is the marrying trap." There was nothing else to do but go for the lowdown kicks of that trap. It's all finished now. The teeth are rusty and the chain's snapped. I'm an old man of ninety-nine and can't get to a hundred.'

'Wait till you're a hundred and can't get back to being twenty-seven,' Freddy smiled. 'You'll like that even less.'

'We'll get bombed before then.'

'Don't bank on it.'

Larry came back, carrying his wide shoulders and freshly shaved round face, black hair plastered down. 'Pass me that box of hubs, Blackclock,' a new man at work once shouted. Larry put down his brush and strolled over: 'What did you say?' The man was just out of the army, tall, spruce and bronzed: 'Give me that box of hubs. I can't waste time. I'm on piecework.' Larry, a foot shorter, looked up at him: 'You called me Blackclock,' he said, deceptively tearful. 'You said: "Pass me that box of hubs, Blackclock." I heard you.' 'Well,' the man said, 'I had to refer to you as something. Come on, be a good chap and pass them hubs.' Isaac stood beside him: 'What's up?' 'This streak of withered piss called me Blackclock. He's a scab' – up to his face that grew more astonished with each insult – 'a screwgut, a gett-face, a rat-eyed dog who thinks he's still in Kenya or Cyprus. "Blackclock," he shouted, and even the women on viewing heard it.'

He greeted them soberly. 'Still slinging 'em down?'

Freddy called for more: 'Jawing, you mean. Isaac

was saying we're as likely to get blown up by American atom bombs as by Russian.'

'It's all the same to me,' Larry said. 'I don't mind the Russians coming, to tell you the truth. As long as they don't send them Mongolian hordes. I wouldn't like them Mongolians raping my wife. I wouldn't fancy that at all.' Isaac spluttered in his beer, a stitch in his stomach as if his appendix had turned into a dum-dum bullet. He had seen Larry's wife once outside the factory, and though he imagined the Mongolians might not be over-particular regarding their women, he failed to see her as anything but safe when they swarmed one fine day over the Trent.

The man's blow pushed Larry against the machine, thickset brawn saving him among levers and spindles. He was geared for the spring-back: 'Hold off,' Isaac said. The foreman had seen it: hadn't the army trained him in team spirit and comradeship? Or were such qualities overridden by a desire to disregard life among dangerous machinery? He told Larry and Isaac not to bother the man, just because he didn't like the idea of joining a union. Isaac swore: as far as he knew the man was in a union already. He'd only stood by to make sure nobody came to harm. The ex-soldier was moved to the packing department.

A fortnight later Larry walked in with a black eye and a graze down the side of his face. 'I punched that bloke up last night.'

'Trust him to make that crack about getting him to join the union,' Isaac said, still brooding on it.

'They've got their hooks into you,' Larry said. They certainly had, thought Isaac. In this life of profit and loss, fighting to keep your wages up, and battling against the ever-increasing threat of the double stint, existence was getting harder. They'd drive you into the ground with that velvet glove if you didn't play the flick-knife now and again. They shoved out the message that you were having it good, all the time making sure you had it worse and worse. Agitation, the lightning strike, the big shout and the black look were always in use, for if one small advantage crept against you the whole line collapsed. People would get laid off for no reason, and the next reduction of hours and increase of the flat rate would be impossible to achieve. The only spiritual unity left to those in the factory was the fight for material conditions. That's what religion had come to, with never an amen among the steel-wool clouds.

'Join the communists, then,' Larry said, as Isaac talked on about it, 'like me.'

'I go around on my own. When the balloon goes up I'll know what to do.'

'I'll just sing,' Larry said.

'I'm too Red to join any party,' Isaac said. 'They'd throw me out if they heard my ideas. I think factories should have MPs, not districts. Only people with insurance cards should vote. That'd be fair.'

'Maybe only those with ration cards,' Freddy said.

Isaac caught his irony: 'Same thing. I could run our factory, though. I've worked in every department and seen the whole process going for years. If I could keep some of the chargehands I'd send that production skyhigh, and people wouldn't drop dead from fatigue either. As for those bastards trying to run it now, I'm always on the lookout for a wall that's long enough to mow them down against. I don't want social justice any more; I want revenge.'

Larry scoffed, 'Why cut your own throat though?'

'The only time that might be possible,' Freddy said, 'is when that four-minute warning goes and the bombs start dropping. And there'll be no four-minute warning given to the public, only to Civil Defence, police and army so that they can be ready for us, man.'

'I was round at Wally Jones's place on the worst night last time,' Isaac said, 'and he's got a German mauser and a couple of shotguns. We were making plans in case there was trouble. I'm going to get a gun. I'm taking no chances. I'll get some Tory bastards before I go, not to mention a few toffee-nosed Labour getts. I shan't die like a cat.'

'The best thing is to make your peace with God.'

'That's what they play on, and expect you not to care.' He was hungry and bought three meat pies, but they were old and stale as if, he said, pushing it aside, they'd been made from pensioned-off pit-ponies. Larry wolfed his down. Freddy ate half: 'It's a sin to waste food. It's feeding the devil.'

'That's what my mother says when anyone slings grub on the fire,' Isaac told him, taking the stomach out of his pint.

'The trouble is,' Larry said, 'you've got no ambition, Isaac. You should have taken that chargehand's job that was offered you. Me, I'll never get anywhere. I know that. But you, you've got it in you. You're just the age for a few steps up in a factory life. If you was just a little bit on their side, the gaffers would pull you in with a golden handshake and fart all over you with pleasure.'

'He's right,' Freddy put in. 'Who sharpens tools when the chargehand's gone for a walk? Isaac. Who fixed my machine in two minutes when it broke down, latched my belt on when it snapped? You think the foreman didn't notice? You'd have been the gaffer's golden-haired boy years ago if you hadn't been such a troublemaker, taking home twenty every week just for things you've been able to do for years.'

Isaac felt, behind his stony face, as if unborn, though nerves jumping and ready to eat him up. Maybe I'm getting a cold, or a bilious bout. Freddy put an arm over his shoulder: 'When I drop in on Thursday I'll let Beatty know where you were last night. My wife took you a cup of cocoa and an extra blanket before you dropped off, pure as driven coal-gas.'

'Maybe I won't need an alibi. Thanks, though.' He stood up and fastened his coat: 'See you on Monday.'

Fresh air knocking out of a blue sky doused him as if after a cold tap-wash. Each footstep took him further from the unrealistic comfort of his friends. He felt raw-hearted in these streets, with no ally but his own self to protect or destroy him. He felt rotten for what happened last night. The way of existence was awful and putrid because it drained life away and gave nothing back. To blame it was useless perhaps, only dodging from the real wound bleeding deep in his purple innards. His life seemed a black dead-end darkness when he looked at things closer than most people cared to. There was no one to blame for this, yet if some new system of social life came to involve him deeply then this piece of stupid personal confusion might bother him less than it did. Such logic seemed incontrovertible – a streamroller decked with trimmings that would set him hand-clapping if ever he saw it in motion.

VI

Saturday was tin-dinner day at Tom and Mary's: tinned peas and tinned steak, followed by tinned rhubarb or rice pudding, with tinned beer to see it through if you felt so inclined – as if for one day a week that acquired the status of explorers lost on some spiritual ice-cap of the world. Though it seemed a tasty enough meal to Mary, Beatty couldn't get through half of it.

Thumbs were down on Isaac, the grating lifted, the lions out. Tom jumped his motor-bike to cruise innumerable districts of the city in which he might be found – a hopeless job, but he went just the same, withdrawing his long hymnal of a head from every smoky pub, as if a dart-player might swing a fine-feathered missile in his direction. The reconnaissance was as much to quieten Beatty as to find Isaac. After all – sliding a crash helmet from the kitchen shelf – he's capable of coming back when and if he feels like it.

Beatty had given him up, could tell it was finished by the hard-as-crystal air, cool and passive. She wanted a long sit-down, with cups of tea and fags. He'd gone, and it didn't bother her a bit, there being worse things than a broken home. It was less than a day, yet seemed like weeks because the solid bedwarming hump had been absent last night, logged up no doubt with some other woman. But how could that be true when they'd been happy for so long? The wild passion had gone out of it, yet love was still there. He had no reason to run away and hide, do it on her, die.

'Don't worry, love, he'll be back – worse luck. Maybe men and women would be better off without marriage and all this facing-things-together stuff.' Beatty didn't think much of Mary for spouting this bit of comfort, felt insulted at her thinking she needed it. It wasn't meant anyway, just said casually because Mary couldn't bear to see anyone upset, being more upset in fact at seeing somebody upset than the person who was really upset. Mary was her sister, ten years more buxom, and born from a different father, so maybe they didn't see things as real sisters should.

'I'm not worrying,' Beatty said, spent fag thrown to the fire. 'I've got so used to feeling safe with him that I can't think anything's wrong. Yet that car worries me.'

'There's no telling how far he's gone in that thing. If I knew he hadn't got in an accident I'd know how to take it. I've finished with him though.'

'Wait and see what's happened,' Mary cautioned. 'He's only gone since last night.'

She shook her head. What was the use? You just stop living until you know: 'Don't tell me to wait and see again, because what else do you think I'm doing?'

Mary was annoyed at the sympathy that wasn't easy being slung back in her face. Hadn't she said many a time that there was no saying when he would go off the rails? It might be lack of opportunity, or will, but the certainty was always there, waiting to do it on her without warning when the shock would be hardest to bear. 'I've got to say something, haven't I?'

'No,' Beatty said, 'you haven't.' She wanted peace, to be left alone. Even the sound of her kids playing in the street with Mary's travestied the pure burning openness of her mind that did not know what to think and kept her on a perch of hope and misery unable even to light another cigarette that she so much wanted. She dreaded the kids bursting in to ruffle this calm death weaving around her, hoped that Tom would come back, that Isaac would kick his way into the room and demand to know why she wasn't at home getting his tea ready, thirsty and famished after spilling a genuine list of misadventures.

She regretted bringing her troubles to Tom and Mary. A lot of good they were when the only comfort possible could be from Isaac. He was a rotter, leaving her like this, and to keep saying it soothed her, as if such words were a magic bait to draw the wandering fish back to her net.

She laughed: sarcasm, bitterness, lack of hope. Mary was startled from the newspaper, angry at her sister's easy surrender to the hard ways of the world. They fastened their claws into everyone's heart and soul, but you couldn't admit that they got you down or made you suffer, since other miseries existed that could make your present state seem a bit of a joke: 'There's worse things at sea,' she said.

'But we aren't at bloody sea,' Beatty snapped. 'You wouldn't be so cheerful if Tom walked out on you.'

'I wouldn't make such a fuss about it. And don't say I don't love him, either. I'd grin and bear it if he lit off.'

'You sound as if you want him to go,' Beatty said, lifted from her troubles by the fascinating snap of conviction in her sister's voice.

Mary's face flushed. 'Trust you to think that. You take everything the wrong way.'

'Except my own troubles,' Beatty said, subdued again. 'I wonder where he's got to? And Tom's been gone hours.'

VII

Rifle Street, Gatling Street, Bastion Street, Redoubt Street, Citadel Street – fighting monickers made up by some fat and comfortable swine who'd never heard a bomb or had a fist in his face. A smart young girl went into a shop with a basket of bottles: Miss Joggletits of nineteen umpty-jump, such smart knockers as he'd ever seen. I'd name them Love Street, Vagina Row, Womb Lane – paint the houses, pave the roadway, disinfect the gutters, change that smashed drainpipe and give the woman there five bob for some glass and putty to mend her window. Where it says Vote for Sludge-bump get a famous artist to paint a bare woman. Tart the place up a bit.

The afternoon was half over, walking among the cobbled streets and inhaling smells of moss, backyards, and fever-grates. The rhythmic tread of still gleaming shoes, the warm lug of his overcoat, and the continual fag-light not too far from his chin, brought back last night's prowl and unexpected adventure. Maybe I come from a family of fornicators, and that's all there is to it. He remembered a story of his long-dead grandfather who at sixty was discovered standing in with the same woman as his married son – such a depth-charge upsetting the placid waters of three generations.

If I'm heading for the knackers' yard I'll go there sober, feel jack-all when the pole-axe drops and sends me slithering into the dream-chute of blood and guts. Fits and fevers, miseries and screams – something's got to give, and it won't be me. I'm twenty-seven, and eighteen was too old to change my habits. When I was thirteen I'd never forget a grudge, and at seventeen I'd always look people in the eye. At twenty-one I got the key of the door, but there's been no deep-down happening in my lowest coal galleries since then. Marriage and kids is nothing to get God on the blower about.

He walked, turning three corners to come in half a minute to the copper's slab back and broach his own car unseen. The weights of his legs, sinews, boot-laces and lungs seemed to hold him from real speed, every footlift needing a steam-hammering piston to generate power in the back of each heel – though he looked smart and full of purpose walking towards himself in a plate-glass window.

Sunlight threw a line of bars along the polished flank of his car. He observed it as if inside a special prison that he was not able to enter. The copper stood at the end of the street, a clear, dark, indisputable toy shape guarding hard-earned glamour from the claws of its rightful owner. He grinned, not so much at the funny situation, as at the sense of waiting for the copper to continue his beat so that he could step along the pavement and steal his roadster without committing a crime, and without showing his papers as proof that it belonged to him.

But the copper only went as far as the corner. Isaac braked, drew back to another stalemate. The copper turned, as if his gimlet-eyes were looking straight at him. A couple of years ago, beaten well into the trough of married blight, he might have been willing to show his licence, and laugh off the forceput of it, but nowadays his back was up, obstinacy permeating every last bay and fibre of his emerging world. Maybe he'd never again see each tenth of a mile registered in orange figurines whose wheel-spins, strictly accounted for, were marked off against his credit.

To see this mileage meant he could either go up directly, and show his papers if necessary, or saunter by and glimpse it from the pavement, risk being recognized. He preferred the policeman to vanish, leave him in freedom to take control of his car, but that wasn't how things worked. God, chance, or fate was an old believer of the hard way, the grinding jewel clipping at the brain until you acted, and took a gamble on whether it worked or not.

A few right-hand turns, and the copper still stood at his accustomed spot. Isaac switched back, en route for what must become his. He took out black, large, horn-rimmed spectacles for driving on rainy nights: distant objects such as dogs and architectural decrepitudes appeared slightly clearer, but the weight was really compensated for by their power of disguise. He drew a thin mustard-coloured cap jauntily over his head, so that from a rough-faced factory worker in his weekend best he became a whipper-featured anglo-intellectual adman trying to look like a sensitive artisan, who knew of a short cut across the slums from one area of good houses to another.

He even felt different but, adding a final touch of incongruous realism, pulled a sawn-off briar from his back pocket and latched it between his teeth. Over a few rows of slate-roofed houses lay a captive car that he hoped to release by the use of outlandish guile. Through a reflecting window he saw the vicious, driving, debonair creation he'd become if he stopped being himself.

The policeman walked by without a glance. Isaac gloated, not even bothering to read the milometer on his car, turned at the end of the street to see the policeman strolling away as if at last to give other properties a fairer share of his protection.

Game successful, tricks finished, he took off cap, pipe and glasses. The click of car-keys going into the lock like Christmas sleigh-bells was drowned by a motor-bike throttling along the street. Isaac saw him first, knelt as if having trouble with the handle and hoping that tin-pot push-button people's bike would pass on the far side and carry his search-party brother-in-law to another zone of fruitlessness. The roar increased, stopped, and Isaac stood slowly, as if under a ceiling only high enough for a dwarf: 'What are you doing round this way?'

He lit a cigarette, as if to say nothing more, knowing Tom had been sent out to bring him back dead or alive, drunk or sober. 'I was just passing,' Tom said, parking his bike by the kerb, 'and saw your car.' He took off his crash-helmet (as advertised on TV) and strode over as if for a long chat, his face like a miner's safety lamp: solid, shining, aware of all dangers, indestructible. 'Beatty happened to mention you hadn't been in all night.'

They faced each other across the bonnet. 'I was with some of my mates,' Isaac said, bending to get in his car. 'We got a bit drunk.'

Tom took his arm: 'Just a bit. You can't go like that.'

He had never liked Beatty's sister, mother, or brother-in-law, saw them as too dull and solid in their sloth, looking on pale normality as blood-curdling life, contemptible dummies trying to drag him down. He pushed Tom away: 'Keep your hands off me or I'll put you in the gutter.'

'You ought to come back to your wife and kids,' Tom said, white-faced at such violence. 'You know how Beatty worries. Why don't you just come and let her see you're all right?'

'Then I can come out again and play? Listen, jam-face, don't act big brother with me.' The wind rattled them. Isaac saw the situation so clearly that the result was confusing. Pictures proliferated like poison-ivy in the brain, gave him a pain in the head.

Tom went on spouting. Rockets of deadly advice sloped towards heaven in threatening colours, and cracker mottoes came down by parachute. He was sorry Isaac wasn't sorry for all the trouble he might be going to cause, and Isaac smiled at this, noticed how he put a hand in his pocket out of nervousness and rattled at his money like a sex-maniac. Tom spoke of how tragic it was that a good marriage should crash for no reason, especially with three beautiful kiddies asking since last night when their dad was coming home. Isaac wanted to laugh, at Tom with glowing eyes and dull conviction saying what crimes Isaac ought not to commit – because Tom had always wanted to get stuck into them but hadn't the guts. 'What shall I tell her?'

'I'll tell her myself.'

'Will you come back now, though?' Tom wanted everything neat, a piece of wedding-cake tied up with blue ribbon, all the happy suffering locked inside. Isaac thought him too hasty, a careful saver out of his element. Tom had always been tidy in mind and dress, even carried it off with a dry sort of humour. You not only had to laugh at his jokes, you had to understand them as well – which often cut the heart out of the laugh. He was the kind of person who would iron his own boot-laces. He wouldn't even let his wife do it.

'You shouldn't let her suffer so,' he said, still anxious.

'I'll be back.'

'I know you like to do things your own way, but come and talk to her yourself.'

'I can't. Tell her not to worry.'

'It ain't that she thinks you've left her. She just wonders where you've got to.'

Isaac saw it beginning all over again, the same words in different order, putting him in the wrong like the lowest worm. 'Get off my back,' he threatened. 'I'll settle things my own way when I'm ready.'

A feline explosion burst from Tom: 'Who do you think you are?'

'If you don't get away from me,' Isaac bellowed, 'I'll wrap that motor-bike round your neck and throttle you with it.'

Maybe the policeman was drawn to the street by their quarrel, or perhaps he'd merely returned to it after a natural lapse of his beat. Isaac had Tom by the strings of his windjammer: 'Get back to your rabbit hutch, you sanctimonious bastard.'

'What's all the argument?' the policeman wanted to know.

Isaac was opening his own car door: 'Having a talk. But it's finished now.'

'I'll say it is,' Tom agreed, his lampface dimming out.

'It sounded a bit more than that to me,' the copper said. 'Is that car yours? You're the chap as was here a couple of hours ago, aren't you?'

'Yes, it is my car,' Isaac told him. 'Ask my brother-in-law.'

Tom was astride his motor-bike, crash-helmet and chinstraps proving ownership: 'I don't know what he's talking about. I just stopped to light a fag.' His foot stamped on the pedal and the engine crowed, hosannahed from one end of the street to the other.

'You'd better show me your papers.'

'Tell him it's mine,' Isaac called.

With a gliding motion Tom was propelled to the middle of the road, showed a straight self-righteous back as he turned the corner.

'I'd like to see them papers,' the copper said.

Even his monument to sweat and thrift was disputed, which at last proved fatally yet to his satisfaction that you had no right to have property at all. Property blacked out your teeth, ploughed lanes of baldness through your hair, turned down your mouth, lopped off your ears, gave you a blinding squint, splayed your nose flat. He owned a car but it compromised his dignity. Even the licence and insurance weren't enough:

'It says the car belongs to Isaac Starbuck, but I'm not to know you're not somebody else, am I? If you've got no more proof than this you can come with me. Maybe we'll help you to find it.'

Half drunk from the shuttling racket of life since last night, Isaac took out his brand-new dark-blue stiff-backed passport. Though not as yet travel worn, it was an impressive certificate to respectability and intentions.

'That's all right,' the policeman said, handing it back, 'we have to keep on our toes, you know. There's been a lot of car thieving lately around this area, even in daytime.'

Isaac got into the car, feeling as if the lights were on him. A black volcanic bile boiling up, he wanted to leave the scene of his defeat quickly, before he spewed over the well-kept upholstery. He spun his car on to the main road. Not yet, not yet, not yet. The bomb has exploded and the smoke goes up. It may drift for weeks or months. But you can't in any case crawl away until the debris has cleared. I can hold myself in now until the time comes. Then I'll walk out of this emptiness in one fine piece, and never come back.

GUZMAN, GO HOME

BOUNCING and engine-noise kept the baby soothed, as if he were snug in the belly of a purring cat. But at the minute of feeding-time he screamed out his eight-week honeyguts in a high-powered lament, which nothing but the nipple could stop. Somewhere had to be found where he could feed in peace and privacy, otherwise his cries in the narrow car threatened the straight arrow on Chris's driving.

He often had fifty miles of road to himself, except when a sudden horn signalled an overtaking fast-driven Volkswagen loaded to the gills. 'Look how marvellously they go,' Jane said. 'I told you you should have bought one. No wonder they overtake you so easily, with that left-hand drive.'

Open scrub fanned out north and west, boulders and olive trees, mountains combing the late May sky of Spain. It was sombre and handsome country, in contrast to the flat-chested fields of England. He backed into an orange grove, red earth newly watered, cool wind coming down from the fortress of Sagunto. While Jane fed the baby, he fed Jane and himself, broke off pieces of ham and cheese for a simultaneous intake to save time.

The car was so loaded that they looked like refugees leaving a city that the liberating army is coming back to. Apart from a small space for the baby the inside was jammed with cases, typewriter, baskets, flasks, coats, umbrellas, and plastic bowls. On the luggage-rack lay a trunk and two cases with, topping all, a folded pram-frame, and collapsible bath.

It was a new car, but dust, luggage, and erratic driving gave it a veteran appearance. They had crossed Paris in a hail and thunderstorm, got lost in the traffic maze of Barcelona, and skirted Valencia by a ring road so rotten that it seemed as if an earthquake had hit it half an hour before. Both wanted the dead useless tree of London lifted off their nerves, so they locked up the flat, loaded the car, and sailed to Boulogne, where the compass of their heart's desire shook its needle towards Morocco.

They wanted to get away from the political atmosphere that saturated English artistic life. Chris, being a painter, had decided that politics ought not to concern him. He would 'keep his hands clean' and get on with his work. 'I like to remember what happened in 1848 to Wagner,' he said, 'who fell in with the revolution up to his neck, helping the workers to storm the arsenal in Dresden, and organizing stores for the defence. Then when the revolution collapsed he hightailed it to Italy to be "entirely an artist" again.' He laughed loud, until a particularly deep pothole cut it short in his belly.

Flying along the straight empty road before Valencia they realized the meaning of freedom from claustrophobic and dirty London, from television and Sunday newspapers, and their middle-aged mediocre friends who talked more glibly nowadays of good restaurants than they had formerly about socialism. The gallery owner advised Chris to go to Majorca, if he must get away, but Chris wanted to be near the mosques and museums of Fez, smoke *kif* at the tribal gatherings of Taroudant and Tafilalt, witness the rose-hip snake-green sunsets of Rabat and Mogador. The art dealer couldn't see why he wanted to travel at all. Wasn't England good enough for other painters and writers? 'They like it here, so why don't you? Travel broadens the mind, but it shouldn't go to the head. It's a thing of the past – old-fashioned. You're socially conscious, so you can't be away from the centre of things for long. What about the marches and sit-downs, petitions, and talks?'

For ten hours he'd driven along the hairpin coast and across the plains of Murcia and Lorca, wanting to beat the previous day's run. They hadn't stopped for the usual rich skins of sausage-protein and cheese, but ate biscuits and bitter chocolate as they went along. He hardly spoke, as if needing all his concentration to wring so many extra miles an hour from the empty and now tolerable road.

His impulse was to get out of Spain, to put that wide arid land behind them. He found it dull, its people too beaten down to be interesting or worth knowing. The country seemed a thousand years older than it had on his last visit. Then, he'd expected insurrection at any time, but now the thought of it was a big horse-laugh. The country smelt even more hopeless than England – which was saying a lot. He wanted to reach Morocco which, no matter how feudal and corrupt, was a new country that might be on the up and up.

So when the engine roared too much for good health at Benidorm, he chose to keep going in order to reach Almeria by nightfall. That extra roar seemed caused by a surcharge of rich fuel at leaving the choke out too long, that would right itself after twenty miles. But it didn't, and on hairpin bends he had difficulty controlling the car. He was careful not to mention this in case his wife persuaded him to get it repaired – which would delay them God knew how many days.

When the plains of Murcia laid a straight road in front of them, it wasn't much after midday. What did hunger matter with progress so good? The roaring of the engine sometimes created a dangerous speed, but maybe it would get them to Tangier. Nothing could be really wrong with a three-month old car – so he drove it into the remotest part of Spain, sublime indifference and sublime confidence blinding him.

He shot through Villa Oveja at five o'clock. The town stood on a hill, so gear had to be changed, causing such a bellowing of the engine that people stared as if expecting the luggage-racked car to go up any second like the Bomb, that Chris had fought so hard to get banned. The speed increased so much that he daren't take his foot from the brake even when going uphill.

The houses looked miserable and dull, a few doorways opening into cobblestoned *entradas*. By one an old woman sat cutting up vegetables; a group of children were playing by another; and a woman with folded arms looked as if waiting for some fast car full of purpose and direction to take her away. Pools of muddy water lay around, though no rain had fallen for weeks. A petrol pump stood like a one-armed veteran of the Civil War outside an open motor workshop – several men busy within at the bonnet of a Leyland lorry. 'These Spanish towns give me the creeps,' he said, hooting a child out of the way.

He waved a farewell at the last house. Between there and Almeria the earth, under its reafforestation skin of cactus and weed, was yellow with sand, desert to be traversed at high speed with eyes half-closed. The road looped the hills, to the left sheer wall and to the right precipices that fell into approaching dusk. Earth and rocks generated a silence that reminded him of mountains anywhere. He almost expected to see snow around the next bend.

In spite of the faulty engine he felt snug and safe in his sturdy car, all set to reach the coast in a couple of hours. The road ahead looked like a black lace fallen from Satan's boot in heaven. No healthy tune was played by the sandy wind, and the unguarded drop on the right was enough to scare any driver, yet kilometres were a shorter measure than miles, would soon roll him into the comfort of a big meal and a night's hotel.

On a steep deserted curve the car failed to change gear. Chris thought it a temporary flash of overheated temper from the clutch mechanism, but, trying again – before the loaded car rolled off the precipice – drew a screech of igniting steel from within the gearbox.

He was stopped from trying the gears once more by a warning yell from Jane, pulled the handbrake firmly up. The car still rolled, its two back wheels at the cliff edge, so he pressed with all his force on the footbrake as well, and held it there, sweat piling out on to the skin of his face. They sat, the engine switched off.

Wind was the only noise, a weird hooting brazen hill-wind from which the sun had already extricated itself. 'All we can do,' he said, 'is hope somebody will pass, so that we can get help.'

'Don't you know *anything* about this bloody car? We can't sit here all night.' Her face was wound up like a spring, life only in her righteous words. It was as if all day the toil of the road had been preparing them for just this.

'Only that it shouldn't have gone wrong, being two months old.'

'Well,' she said, 'British is best. You know I told you to buy a Volkswagen. What do you *think* is wrong with it?'

'I don't know. I absolutely don't bloody well know.'

'I believe you. My God! You've got the stupidity to bring me and a baby right across Europe in a car without knowing the first thing about it. I think you're mad to risk all our lives like this. You haven't even got a proper driving licence.' The wind, too, moaned its just rebuke. But the honeyed sound of another motor on the mountain road filtered into the horsepower of their bickering. Its healthy and forceful noise drew closer, a machine that knew where it was going, its four-stroke cycle fearlessly cutting through the silence. While he searched for a telling response to her tirade, Jane put her arm out, waving the car to stop.

It was a Volkswagen (of course, he thought, it bloody well had to be), a field-grey low-axled turtle with windows, so fresh-washed and polished that it might just have rolled off the conveyor line. Its driver leaned out while the engine still turned: '*Que ha pasado*?'

Chris told him: the car had stopped, and it wasn't possible to change gear, or get it going at all. The Volwagen had a Spanish number plate, and the driver's Spanish, though grammatical, was undermined by another accent. He got out, motioned Chris to do the same. He was a tall, well-built man dressed in khaki slacks and a light-blue open-necked jersey-shirt a size too small: his chest tended to bulge through it and gave the impression of more muscle than he really had. His bare arms were tanned, and on one was a small white mark where a wristwatch had been. There was a more subtle tan to his face, as if it had done a slow change from lobster red to a parchment colour, oil-soaked and wind-worn after a lot of travel.

To Chris he seemed like a rescuing angel, yet there was a cast of sadness, of disappointment underlying his face that, with a man of his middle-age, was no passing expression. It was a mark that life had grown on him over the years, and for good reason, since there was also something of great strength in his features. As if to deny all this – yet in a weird way confirming it more – he had a broad forehead, and the eyes and mouth of an alert benign cat, and like so many short-sighted Germans who wore rimless spectacles he had that dazed and distant look that managed to combine stupidity and ruthlessness.

He sat in the driver's seat, released the brake, and signalled Chris to push. *'Harémos la vuelta.'*

Jane stayed inside, rigid from the danger they had been in, weary in every vein after days travelling with a baby that was feeding from herself. She turned now and again to tuck the sheet under the baby. The man beside her deftly manoeuvred the car to the safe side of the road, and faced it towards the bend leading back to Villa Oveja.

He started the engine. The turnover was healthy, and the wheels moved. Chris saw the car sliding away, wife, luggage, and baby fifty yards down the road. He was too tired to be afraid they would vanish for ever and leave him utterly alone in the middle of these darkening peaks. He lit a cigarette, in a vagrant slap-happy wind that, he had time to think, would never have allowed him to do so in a more normal situation.

The car stopped, then started again, and the man tried to change gear, which brought a further roaring screech from the steel discs within. He stopped the car, leaned from the window and looked with bland objective sadness at Chris. Hand on the wheel, he spoke English for the first time, but in an unmistakable German accent. He grinned and said, a high-pitched rhythmical rise and fall, a telegraphic rendering of disaster that was to haunt Chris a long time:

'England, your car has snapped!'

11

'Lucky for you, England, I am the owner of the garage in Villa Oveja. A towing-rope in my car will drag you there in five minutes.

'My name is Guzman – allowing me to introduce myself. If I hadn't come along and seen your break-up you would perhaps have waited all night, because this is the loneliest Iberian road. I only come this way once a week, so you are double lucky. I go to the next town to see my other garage branch, confirm that the Spaniard I have set to run it doesn't trick me too much. He is my friend, as far as I can have a friend in this country where, due to unsought-for happenings, I have spent nearly the same years as my native Germany. But I find my second garage is not doing too wrong. The Spaniards are good mechanics, a very adjustable people. Even without spare parts they have the genius to get an engine living – though under such a system it can't last long before being carried back again. Still, they are clever. I taught my mechanics all I know: I myself was once able to pick tank engines into morsels, under even more trying conditions than here. I trained mechanics well, and answered by taking his knowledge to Madrid, where I don't doubt he got an excellent job – the crooked, ungrateful. He was the most brainful, so what could he do except trick me? I would have done the same in his place. The others, they are fools for not escaping with my knowledge, and so they will never get on to the summit. Likewise they aren't much use for me. But we will fix your car good once we get right back to the town, have no fear of it.

'You say it is only three months old? Ah, England, no German car would be such a bad boy after three months. This Volkswagen I have had two years, and not a nut and bolt has slipped out of place. I never boast about myself, but the Volkswagen is a good car, that any rational human being can trust. It is made with intelligence. It is fast and hard, has a marvellous honest engine, that sounds to last a thousand years pulling through these mountains. Even on scorched days I like to drive with all my windows shut-closed, listening to the engine nuzzling swift along like a happy cat-bitch. I sweat like rivers, but the sound is beautiful. A good car, and anything goes wrong, so you take the lid off, and all its insides are there for the eye to see and the hand-spanner to work at. Whereas your English cars are difficult to treat with. A nut and bolt loose, a pipe snapped, and if you don't burn the fingers you surely sprain the wrist trying to get at the injured fix. It's as if your designers hide them on purpose. Why? It isn't rational why, in a people's car that is so common. A car should be natural to expose and easy to understand. On the other hand you can't say that because a car is new nothing should happen to it. Even an English car. That is unrealistic. You should say: This car is new, therefore I must not let anything happen to it. A car is a rational human being like yourself.

'Thank you. I've always had a wanton for English cigarettes, just as I have for the language. The tobacco is more subtle than the brutal odours of the Spanish. Language is our best lanes of communication, England, and whenever I meet travellers like yourself I take advantage from it.

'You don't like the shape of the Volkswagen? Ah, England! That is the prime mistake in choosing a car. You English are so aesthetic, so biased. When I was walking through north Spain just after the war – before the ink was dry on the armistice signatures, ha, ha! – I was very poor and had no financial money – and in spite of the beautiful landscapes and marvellous towns with walls and churches, I sold my golden spectacles to a bruto farmer so that I can buy sufficing bread and sausage to feed me to Madrid. I didn't see the pleasant things so clearly, and being minus them the print in my Baedeker handbook blurred my eyes, but here I am today. So what does the shape of a car mean? That you like it? That you don't wear spectacles yet, so you'll never have to sell them, you say? Oh, I am laughing. Oh, oh, oh! But England, excuse me wagging the big finger at you, but one day you may not be so fortunate.

'Ah! So! Marvellous, as you say: clever Guzman has flipped into second gear, and maybe I do not need my towing rope to get you back to town. I don't think you were so glad in all your life to meet a German, were you, England? Stray Germans like me are not so current in Spain nowadays.'

Shadows took the place of wind. A calm dusk slunk like an idling panther from the hips and peaks of the mountains. A few yellow lamps shone from the outlying white houses of Villa Oveja. Both cars descended the looping road, then crept up to these lights like prodigal moths.

As he stopped outside Guzman's garage, Chris remembered his ironic goodbye of an hour ago. A small crowd gathered, who'd perhaps witnessed other motorists give that final contemptuous handwave, only to draggle back in this forlorn manner. God's judgement, I suppose they think, the religious bastards. Guzman finished his inspection, sunlight seeming to shine on his glasses even in semi-darkness – which also hid what might be a smile: 'England, I will take you to a hotel where you can stay all night – with your wife and child.'

'All night!' Chris had expected this, so his exclamation wasn't so sharp.

'Maybe two whole nights, England.'

Jane's words were clipped with hysteria: 'I won't spend two nights in this awful dump.' The crowd recognized the livelier inflections of a quarrel, grew livelier themselves. Guzman's smile was less hidden: 'Rationally speaking, it must be difficult travelling with a family-wife. However, you will find the Hotel Universal modest but comfortable, I'm sure.'

'Listen,' Chris said, 'can't you fix this clutch tonight?' He turned to Jane: 'We could still be in Almeria by twelve.'

'Forget it,' she said. 'This is what...'

'... comes of leaving England with a car you know nothing about? Oh for God's sake!'

Guzman's heavy accent sometimes rose to an almost feminine pitch, and now came remorselessly in: 'England, if I might suggest...'

The hotel room smelled of carbolic and Flit; it was scrupulously clean. Every piece of luggage was unloaded and stacked on the spacious landing of the second floor – a ramshackle heap surrounded by thriving able-bodied aspidistras. The room dosed so heavily with Flit gave Jane a headache. Rooms with bath were non-existent, but a handbasin was available, and became sufficient during their three days there.

Off the squalor of the main road were narrow, cobblestoned streets. White-faced houses with overhanging balconies were neat and well cared for. The streets channelled you into a spacious square, where the obligatory church, the necessary town hall, and the useful *telegrafos*, emphasized the importance of the locality. While Guzman's tame mechanics worked on the car Chris and Jane sat in the cool dining room and listened to Guzman himself. On either side of the door leading to the kitchen were two bird cages, as large as prisons, with an austere primitive beauty about the handiwork of them. In each was a hook-beaked tropical bird, and while he talked Guzman now and again rolled up a ball of bread that was left over from dinner and threw it with such swift accuracy at the cage that it was caught by the scissor-beak that seemed eternally poked without.

'I come here always for an hour after lunch or dinner,' he said, lighting a small cigar, 'to partake coffee and perhaps meet interesting people, by which I signify any foreigner who happens to be moving through. As you imagine, not many stay in our little God-forgotten town – as your charming and rational wife surmised on your precipitant arrival here. My English is coming back the more I talk to you, which makes me happy. I read much, to maintain my vocabulary, but speech is rare. I haven't spoken it with anyone for fourteen months. You express motions of disbelief? It's true. Few motorists happen to break up at this particular spot in Spain. Many English who come prefer the coasts. Not that the mosquitoes are any lesser there than here. Still, I killed that one: a last midnight blackout for the little blighter. Ah, there's another. There, on your hand. Get it, England. Bravo. You are also quick. They are not usually so bad, because we Flit them to death.

'I suppose the English like Spain in this modern epoch because of its politics, which are on the right side – a little primitive, but safe and solid. Excuse me, I did not know you were speeding through to Africa, and did not care for political Spain. Not many visit the artistic qualities of Iberia, which I have always preferred. You are fed up with politics, you say, and want to leave them all behind? I don't blame you. You are wisdom himself, because politics can make peril for a man's life, especially if he is an artist. It is good to do nothing but paint, and good that you should not linger among this country. Why does an artist sit at politics? He is not used to it, tries his hand, and then all is explosioned in him. Shelley? Yes, of course, but that was a long time ago, my dear England. Excuse me again, yes, I will have a *coñac*. When I was in London, in 1932, somebody taught me a smart toast: health, wealth, and stealth! *Gesundheit!*

'Forgive my discretion, England, but I see from your luggage that you are an artist, and I must talk of it. I have a great opinion of artists, and can see why it is that your car broke down. Artists know little of mechanical things, and those that do can't ever be great artists. I myself began as a middling artist. It is a long story, which starts when I was eighteen, and I shall tell you soon.

'Your car is in good hands. Don't worry. And you, madam, I forbid you. We can relax after such a dinner. My mechanics have taken out the engine, and are already shaping off the spare necessary on the lathe. There are no spare parts for your particular name of car in this section of Spain, therefore we have to use our intelligent handicraft – to make them from nothing, from scrape, as you say. That doesn't daunt me, England, because in Russia I had to make spare parts for captured tanks. Ah! I learned a lot in Russia. But I wish I hadn't ever been there. My fighting was tragical, my bullets shooting so that I bleed to death every night for my perpetrations. But bygones are bypassed, and are a long time ago. At least I learned the language. *Chto dyelaets?*

'Well, it is a pity you don't have a Volkswagen, which I have all the spare pieces for. Yet if *you'd* had a Volkswagen we wouldn't have been talking here. You would have been in Marrakech. Like my own countrymen: they overtake every traveller on the road in their fast Volkswagens, as if they departed Hamburg that morning and have to get the ferry ship for Tangier this evening, so as to be in Marrakech tomorrow. Then after a swift weekend in the Atlas Mountains they speed back to the office work for another economic miracle, little perceiving that I am one of those that made that miracle possible. What do I mean? How?

'Ah, ah, ah! You are sympathetic. When I laugh loud, so, you don't get up and walk away. You don't stare at me or flinch. Often the English do that, especially those who come to Spain. Red-faced and lonely, they stare and stare, then walk off. But you understand my laugh, England. You smile even. Maybe it is because you are an artist. You say it is because I am an artist? Oh, you are so kind, so kind. I have been an artist and a soldier both, also a mechanic. Unhappily I have done too many things, fallen between cleft stools.

'But, believe it or not, I earned a living for longer years by my drawing than I have done as a garage man. The first money I earned in my life was during my student days in Königsberg – by drawing my uncle who was a ship-captain. My father wanted me to be a lawyer but I desired to be an artist. It was difficult to shake words with my father at that time, because he had just made a return from the war and he was very dispirited about Germany and himself. Therefore he wanted me to obey him as if I had lost the war for him, and he wouldn't let me choose. I had to give up all drawing and become a lawyer, nothing less. I said no. He said yes. So I departed home. I walked twenty miles to the railway station with all the money I'd saved for years, and when I got there, the next day, it transpires that the young fortune I thought I had wouldn't even take me on a mile of my long journey. All my banknotes were useless, yet I asked myself how could that be, because houses and factories still stood up, and there were fields and gardens all around me. I was flabbergasted. But I set off for Berlin with no money, and it took me a month to get there, drawing people's faces for slices of bread and sausage. I began to see what my father meant, but by now it was too late. I had taken the jump, and went hungry for it, like all rebellious youths.

'In my native home-house I had been sheltered from the gales of economy, because I saw now how the country was. Destituted. In Frankfurt a man landed at my foot because he had dropped from a lot of floors up. England, it was terrible: the man had worked for forty years to save his money, and he had none remaining. Someone else ran down the street screaming: "I'm ruined! Ruined utterly!" But all those other shop-keepers who would be ruined tomorrow turned back to their coffee and brandy. No one was solid, England. No solidarity anywhere. Can your mind imagine it? In such a confusion I decided more than ever that the only term one could be was an artist. Coming from Königsberg to Berlin had shown me a thrill for travel. But Berlin was dirty and dangerous. It was full of people singing about socialism – not national socialism, you understand, but communist socialism. So I soon left and went to Vienna – walking. You must comprehend that all this takes months, but I am young, and I like it. I do not eat well, but I did eat, and I have many adventures, with women especially. I think that it was the best time of my life. You want to go, madam? Ah, good night. I kiss your hand, even if you do not like my prattle. Goodnight, madam, good night. A charming wife, England.

'I didn't like Vienna, because its past glories are too past, and it was full of unemployed. One of the few sorts of people I can't like are the people without work. They make my stomach ill. I am not rational when I see them, so I try not to see them as soon as I can. I went to Budapest, walking along the banks of the Danube with nothing except a knapsack and a stick, free, healthy, and young. I was not the old-fashioned artist who sits gloomily starving in his studio-garret, or talks all day in cafés, but I wanted to get out among the world of people. But in every city there was much conflict, where maybe people were finishing off what they had started in the trenches. I watched the steamers travelling by, always catching me up, then leaving me a long way back, until all I could listen was their little toots of progress from the next switch of the river. The money crashed, but the steamers went on. What else could Germany do? It was a good time though, England, because I never thought of the future, or wondered where I would be in the years to reach. I certainly didn't see that I should throw so much of my good years in this little Spanish town – in a country even more destituted than the one in Germany after I set off so easily from my birth-home. Excuse me, if I talk so much. It is the brandy, and it is also making me affectionate and sentimental. People are least intelligent when most affectionate, so forgive me if I do not always keep up the high standard of talk that two artists should kindle among them.

'No, I insist that it is my turn this time. Your wife has gone, no, to look after the baby? In fact I shall order a bottle of brandy. This Spanish liquid is hot, but not too intoxicating. Ah! I shall now pour. It's not that I have the courage to talk to you only when I am up to my neck in bottle-drink, as that I have the courage to talk to you while you are drunk. You can drink me under the table, England? Ah! We shall see, dear comrade. Say when. I have travelled a long way, to many places: Capri, Turkey, Stalingrad, Majorca, Lisbon, but I never foresaw that I should end up in the awkward state I am now in. It is unjust, my dear England, unjust. My heart becomes like a flitterbat when I think that the end is so close.

'Why? Ah! Where was I? Yes. In Budapest there was even more killing, so I went to Klausenburg (I don't know which country that town is in any more) and passed many of these beautiful clean Saxon towns. The peasants wore their ancient pictorial costume, and on the lonely dusty road were full of friendships and dignity. We spoke to each other, and then went on. I walked through the mountains and woods of Transylvania, over the high Carpathians. The horizons changed every day; blue, purple, white, shining like the sun; and on days when there were no horizons because of rain or mist I stayed in some cowshed, or the salon of a farmhouse if I had pleased the family with my sketching likenesses. I went on, walking, walking (I walked every mile, England, a German pilgrim), across the great plain, through Bucharest and over the Danube again, and into Bulgaria. I had left Germany far behind, and my soul was liberal. Politics didn't interest me, and I was amazed, in freedom at my father being sad at the war.

'How the brandy goes! But I don't get drunk. If only I could get drunk. But the more brandy I drink the colder I get, cool and icy on the heart. Even good brandy is the same. Health, wealth, and stealth! I got to Constantinople, and stayed for six months. Strangely, in the poorest city of all, I made a good living. In an oriental city unemployment didn't bother me: it seemed natural. I went around the terraces of hotels along the Bosphorus making portraits of the clientèles, and of all the money I made I gave the proprietors ten per cent. If they were modern I drew them or their wives also against the background of the Straits, and sometimes I would take a commission to portray a palace or historic house.

'One day I met a man who questioned if I would draw a building for him a few kilometres along the coast. He would give me five English pounds now, and five more when we came back to the hotel. Of course I accepted, and we drove in his car. He was a middle-aged Englishman, tall and formal, but he'd offered me a good price for the hour's drawing necessary. By now I had developed the quickness of draughtsmanship, and sat on the headland easily sketching the building on the next cape. While I worked your Englishman, England, walked up and down smoking swiftly on a cigar, and looked nervous about something. I had ended, and was packing my sketches in, when two Turkish soldiers stood from behind a rock and came to us with rifles sticking out. "Walk to the car," the Englishman said to me, hissing, "as if you haven't done anything."

'"But," I said, "we've made nothing – wrong truly."

'"I should say not, my boy," he told me. "That was a Turkish fort you just sketched."

'We run, but two more soldiers stand in front of us, and the Englishman joked with them all four, patted them on the savage head, but he had to give out twenty pounds before they let us go, and then he cursed all the way back.

'It might have been worse, I realize at the hotel, and the Englishman is pleased, but said we'll have to move on for our next venture, and he asked me if I'd ever thought of hiking to the frontier of Turkey and Russia. "Beautiful, wild country," he told me. "You'll never forget it. *You* go there on your own, and make a few sketches for me, and it'll prove lucrative – while I sit back over my sherbet here. Ha, ha, ha!"

'So I questioned him: "Do you want me to sketch Turkish forts, or Soviet ones?"

' "Well," he said, "both."

'That, England, was my first piece of stealthy work, but it never made me wealthy, and I already was healthy. Ah, ah, ah, ho, ho! You are strong, England. I cannot make you flinch when I hit you on the back like a friend. So! Before then I had been too naïve to feel dishonest. Once on the Turkish border I was captured, with my sketches, and nearly hanged, but my Englishman pays money, and I go free. Charming days. I wasn't even interested in politics.

'I hear a baby crying. What a sweet sound it is! England, I think your wife calls for you.'

III

'It is fine night tonight, England, a beautiful star-dark around this town. I have travelled most of my life. Even without trouble I would have travelled, never possessing one jot of wealth, only needing food at the sunset and hot water for breakfast. During the war my voyaging was also simple.

'In my youth, after I was exported from Turkey by the soldiers. (They took all my money before letting me go. If only we had conquered them during the war, then I would have met them again and made them repay it with every drop of their blood!) I travelled in innumerous countries of the Balkans and Central East, until I was so confused by the multiple currencies that I began to lose count of the exchange. I would recite my travellers' cataclysm as I crossed country limits: "Ten Slibs equals one Flap; a hundred Clackies makes one Golden Crud; four Stuks comes out at one Drek" – but usually I went to the next nation with not Slib Flap Clackie or Golden Crud to my name, nothing except what I wear and a pair of worn sandals. I joke about the currencies, because there is no fact I cannot remember. Some borders I have crossed a dozen times, but even so far back I can memory the dates of them, and stand aside to watch myself at that particular time walking along, carefreed, towards the customs post.

'One of my adventures is that I get married, and my wife is a strong and healthy girl from Hamburg who also likes the walking life. Once we trampled from Alexandria, stepping all along the coast of Africa to Tangier, but it was hard because the Mussulmans do not like to have their faces drawn. However, there were many white people we met, and I also sketch a lot of buildings and interesting features – which were later found to be of much use to certain circles in Berlin. You understand, eh?

'We went back to Germany, and walked in that country also. We joined groups of young people on excursions to the Alps, and had many jolly times on the *hohewege* of the Schwarzwald. My wife had two children, both boys, but life was still carefreed. There were more young people like ourselves to enjoy it with. My art was attaining something, and I did hundreds of drawings, all of which made me very proud, though some were better than others, naturally. Most were burned to cinders by your aeroplanes, I am sad to say. I also lost many of my old walking friends in that war, good men ... but that is all in the past, and to be soonest forgotten. Nowadays I have only a few comrades, in Ibiza. Life can be very sad, England.

'In that time before the war my drawings were highly prized in Germany. They hung in many galleries, because they showed the spirit of the age – of young people striving in all their purity to build the great state together, the magnificent corporation of one country. We were patriotic, England, and radical as well. Ah! It is good when all the people go forward together. I know many artists who thought that anarchism was not enough to cure the griefs of the globe as they swung into black shirts. Children do not like the dark when they go to bed, and what can blame them? Someone has to build a fire and put on lights. But you shouldn't think I liked the bad things though, about inferior races and so on. Because if you consider, how could I be living in Spain if I did? It was a proud and noble time when loneliness was forgotten. It contained sensations I often spend my nights thinking about, because I felt that after all the travels of my young days I was getting at last some look-on at my work, as well as finding the contentment of knowing a leader who pointed to me the fact that I was different from those people I had been through on my travels. He drew me together. Ah! England, at that you get more angry than if I had banged you on the shoulder like a jolly German! You think I am so rotten that when I cut myself, maggots run out. But don't, please don't, because I can't stand that from any man. I don't believe anything now, so let me tell you. Nothing, nothing... nothing. Everyone was joining something in those days, and I couldn't stop myself, even though I was an artist. And because I was an artist I went the whole way, to the extremes, right beyond the nether boundaries. I was carried along like this *coñac* cork, floating down a big river. I couldn't swim out of it, and in any case the river was so strong that I liked it, I liked being in it, a strong river, because I was as light as a cork, and it would never carry me under. He ... he made us as light as a cork, England. But politics are gone from my life's vision. I make no distinction any more between races or systems. One of my favourite own jokes is that of Stalin, Lenin and Trotsky playing your money game Monopoly together in the smallest back room of the Kremlin in 1922. Ha, ha, ha! You also think it is funny, England, no?

'No, you don't think it is funny, I can see that. I am sorry you don't. Your face is stern and you are gazing far away. But listen to me though, you are lucky. So far you don't know what it is to belong to a nation that has taken the extreme lanes, but you will, you will. So I can see it coming because I read your newspapers. Up till now your country has been lucky, ours has been unlucky. We had no luck, none at all. We are rational, intelligent, strong, but unlucky. You cut off the head of your King Karl; we didn't of our Karl. Ah, now you smile at my wit. You laugh. You have the laugh of the superior, England, the mild smile of those who do not know, but once on a time, if any foreigner laughed at me like that I could kill them. And I did! I did!

'Stop me if I shout. Forgive me. No, don't go, England. Your baby is not crying. Your wife does not call. Listen to me more. I don't believe anything except that I am able to repair your car and do it good. And that is something. How many men can set you on the road again? It is a long way from my exhibitions of drawings, one of which, at Magdeburg, was opened and appreciated by You-know-who, a person who also knew about art. Yes, actually him. He shook my own hand, this hand! I was reconciled to my father by then: I who hated my father more than any hatred that was ever possible since the beginnings of the civilized world was brought back to respect him, to view his point with proper sympathy. To be able to again give respect to one's father in middle-age! Can you imagine it ever, England? And who did it? He is truly a great man who can make the different generations understand each other, a dictator maybe, but great, still a genius. I tell you that my father was the proudest man in all Germany because he who had done it had shaken this – this hand!

'Well, I will not ennui you any more about my adventures in those days. Let us skip a few years and talk about romantic Spain. Not that it was romantic. It can be a very dirty place, and annoying, unlike the cleaner countries, such as ours, my dear England. Just after crossing the mountains on foot in 1945, I stayed in a shepherd's hut for two weeks of hiding. Someone paid the shepherd a terrible high rent for this stenching sty, and all the while I was attacked by ants, so that I go nearly mad. I looked mad – with my long beard and poor clothes, dreamed I was the King of Steiermark with my loptilted crown. Ants came in the door, and I start to kill them with hammer and sceptre – then I spare some lives in the hope that they would scuttle back and tell their friends that they had better not come near that hut because a crazy bone-German is conducting a proficient massacre. But it made no difference, and they kept coming on into the kill-feast. I worked for days to stop them, but they came continuously I suppose to see why it was that those before them were not coming back. There were thousands, and my romantic nature won because I got tired first. Strength and intelligence finally let me down. Ants are inhuman. Nowadays, if I see ants in my house or garage I use a Flit gun – bacteriological warfare, if you like, and that is quicker. I can let science take over and so don't need to beg stupid questions. It stops them. I think of all those poor ants who get killed, and maybe the ants themselves have no option but to start this war on me. If only they were all individuals, England, like you – or me – then maybe only one or two would have been killed before the others turned and ran. But no, they have their statues to the war, the Tomb of the Unknown Ant, who dies so that every ant could have his pebble of sugar, but who died in vain, of course. I have a sense of humour? Yes, I have. But it didn't protect me from doing great wrongs.

'How did I get to Spain? My life is full of long stories, but this time I came to Spain from necessity, from dire necessity. It was a matter of life and death. To get here I set out from Russia on a journeying much longer than the one I told you about already in my youth. Name a country, and I have been in it. Say a town and I can call the main street, because I have slept on it. I can tell you about the colour of the policeman's uniform, and where you can get the cheapest food; which is the best corner to stand and ask for money. I have done many things since the end of the war that I would not naturally do, that I should be ashamed of, except that it is man's duty to survive. And man's duty to let him? you said. Of course, quite right, quite so. Humanitarian people are right next door to my heart, my dear friend. But during the war I thought men couldn't survive, and when the war started to end I taught myself that they could. How did I come to obtain my garage business? you ask. It takes much money to buy a garage, and I tell you something now that I wouldn't tell a walking soul, not even my wife, so that instead of forgiving me, you will try to understand.

'I got to Algeria. To say how would damage a few people, so I mustn't. Part of my time I was a teacher of English in Setif, and passed myself as an Englishman. I imitated in every manner that man who was a spy back on the Turkish Bosphorus until nobody in this new place spied the difference. I taught English to Moslems as well, but earned a bad living at it. To augment my inmoney I made intricate maps of farmers' land in the area. I am a good reconnaissance man, and if a farmer had only a very poor and tiny square of land the map I drew made it look like a kingdom, and he was glad to have it square-framed, see something to fight for as he gazed at it hanging on the wall of his tinroofed domicile, at night when the mosquitoes bit him mad, and he was double mad worrying about crops, money, and drought – not to mention rebellion. Then I began selling plots of land in the *bled* that weren't accurately possessed by me – to Frenchmen who came straight out of the army from the mix-in of Indo-China – by telling people it was rich with oil. Nowadays I hear that it really is, but no matter. I sold the land only cheap, but I soon had enough real finance to buy many passports and escape to Majorca. I got fine work as a travel-agent clerk in Palma, and worked good for a year, trying to save my money like an honest man. Spain was a stone country to make a living in then – things are much easier these days since the peseta is devalued. I couldn't save, because all the time I had before me the remembering of the man in Frankfurt who dropped at my feet completely dead because his life savings wouldn't buy a postal stamp. But then an Italian asks me to look after his yacht one winter, which for him was a huge mistake, because when I had sold it to a rich Englishman I took an aeroplane to Paris.

'There I thought I had done such a deal of travelling

in my scattered life that I should turn such knowing into my own business. To commence, I announced in a good newspaper that ten people were desired for a trip around the world, that it would be a co-operative venture, and that only little money would be needed, comparatively. When I saw the ten people I told that two thousand dollars each would be enough, but they had to be fed-up sufficiently with modern world-living to qualify for my expedition. I explained that out of our collective money we would comprise a lorry, and a moving-camera to take documentary films of strange places, that we would sell. Everybody said it was a shining brainwave, and I soon got the lorry and camera cheap. For two weeks we had map meetings while I planned each specific of the trip. I spent as much money on maps as on the lorry, almost, and pinned them to the wall at these gatherings. I gave them labour of cartography and collecting stores. They were all good people, so trusted me, even when I said that a supplementary cost would be laid because of the high price of film. No one would be leader of the expedition, I stipulated: it would be run by committee, with myself as the chairman. But somehow, and against my will, I achieved control. Because I was more interested in getting reactions from other people than from myself I became the real leader of them. In this aspect my good heart triumphed, because they needed me to be their overboss.

'Much of the money I put in the bank, but the peril was I began to like the idea of this world-round journey so much that I couldn't make myself disappear with it. I kept on, obsessed at the plan. I wrote to many shops and factories and (even in France) they gave me equipment. I charged it all to my clients – as I called them in my secret self. Unfortunately the newspaper wrote stories about my scheme, and put my photo in the print.

'So our big lorry set out of Paris, and snapped on the road to Marseilles. I repaired it, and from Marseilles our happy gathering steamed to Casablanca on a packet-boat. I had moved battalions of men and tanks (and many prisoners) in every complication over the eye-dust and soul-mud and numb snow of Russia, but this was a happy situation with these twenty people (by this time others had been entered to our committee). It was like being young again. Everyone loved me. I was *popular*, England, by total consent of all those dear, good friends. Tears fall into my eyes when I think of it – real tears that I can't bear the taste of. The further I gave in to my sentimental journeying and went on with my dear international companions, the less was the money that I intended to go off and begin my garage with in Spain. I had never had such a skirmish in my conscience. What could I do? Tell me, England, what could I do? Would you have done any better than such? No, you wouldn't, I know. My God! I am shouting again. Why don't you stop me?

'The lorry snapped awfully, at Colomb-Bechar, just before we intend to cross the real desert. But my talents triumph again, and I repaired it, and say I am going to try it out. They are still in the tents, eating some lunch, and I drive off, round and round in big circles. Suddenly I make a straight line and they never see me again. I don't know what became of them. They were nearly penniless. I took petrol and the cameras, everything expensive, as well as funds. It is too painful for me to speculate, so ask me nothing else, even if I tell you. From Casablanca I come to here, and when I have collected all from my banks I see there is enough to get my garage, and much to spare.

'And now I am in Spain, you think I have as much as a man could want? I have a Spanish wife, two children and an interesting work. I have had several wives, and now a Spanish woman. She is dark, beautiful, and plump (yes, you have seen her) but in bed she doesn't act with me. My children go to the convent school, and kiss crosses, tremble at nuns and priests. These I cannot like at all, but what can I do? It has been a dull life, because there's not much here. Sometimes we go to a bullfight. But I don't like it. It is a good ritual, but not attractive to a rational human being like myself. All winter we see no travellers, and hug the fireplace like damp washing. Now and again I still do some drawings. Yes, that is one of them over there, that I presented to this hotel. You don't like it? You do? Ah, you make me very happy, England. Often I go down the coast road to Algeciras, a short trip in my dependable Volkswagen. It is a very pleasant port, and I make many sketches. I know some Russians who have a hotel and let me stay at cost rate. Gibraltar is a fascinating shape to make on paper, which I see from the terrace. I also go across to your famous English fort-rock to shopping, and maybe purchase one of those intellectual English Sunday newspapers there. One of them lasts me a month at least. I find them very good, exceptionally lively and interesting to a mind like mine.

'Ah, England, let us take a walk and I will tell you why my life is finished. That's better. The air smells fresh and good. Why, we have talked the whole night through. I tell lies to everyone – with no exception. But to myself – and I talk free to you and myself now – I tell the precise ice-cold truth as far as it is possible. Telling lies to everyone else makes it more possible to tell a more accurate truth to myself. Does that make me happy? For most people happiness is letting them follow the habits their fathers developed. But *he* changed all that, that's why we loved him, drilled truths into us so that we didn't need to live by habit. That would be worse than death – because death is at least something positive.

'That green speck in the sky over there is the first dawn, a little light, a glow-worm that the sun sends in front to make sure that all is dark for it. Your wife will never forgive you. But women are not rational human beings. Oh, oh, oh – England, you think they are? I can prove to you that they are not so, quicker than you can prove to me that they are. You say that the sun is a red sun? I can see that it will be. But I have been in Spain many times. In 1934 I came here, walking all through, sketching farmhouses and touristic monuments – later published as an album in Berlin. I surveyed the land. Spain I know exceedingly well. This beautiful land we saved from Bolshevism – though I sometimes wonder why. I am afraid of a communist government here, because if it comes, I am ended. The whole world gets dark for me. Maybe Franco will make a pact with communist Germany, and send me back to it. It has happened before. I feel my bed is not so safe to lie on.

'My life has been tragic, but I am not one of those who self-pities. It will be hot today. I sweat already. I must sell my garage and leave, go to another country. I am forced to abandon my wife and children, which is not a good fate. It gives me suffering in the heart that you cannot imagine. I am slowly taking secret luggage to my other garage, and one day I shall tell her I'm going to inspect things over there, and she will never see me again. I travel lightly, England, but I am nearly sixty years. You will notice that I have not talked about the war, because it is too hurtful to me. My home was in East Prussia: but the Soviets took the family land.

They enslaved and murdered my fellow countrymen. England, don't laugh. You say they should keep the Berlin Wall there for ever? Ah, you don't know what you are saying. I can see that my misfortune makes you glad. I was not there, of course, but I know what the Soviets did. My wife was killed in one of their bombardments.

'England, please, do not ask me that question. I do not know who started such wicked bombings of the mass. A war begins, and many things happen. Much water flows under the bridge-road. Let me march on with my story. Please, patience. My two sons are in the communist party. As if that was why I fought, used in my body and soul the most terrible energies for one large Germany. I want to go there and beat them both, beat them without mercy, hit at them until they are dead.

'Once I had a letter from them, and they ask me to come back to my homeland – not fatherland, but homeland. How the letter gets me I don't know, but a person in Toledo sends it. They beg me to come back and work for democratic Germany. Why do you think they ask me this? That they are innocent, and only love their father as sons should? Ah! It's because they know I shall be hanged when I get there. That is why they ask. They are devils, devils.

'I am leaving Villa Oveja, quitting Spain, because someone came to this town a few weeks ago and saw me. I think from my photo in the Paris paper and other photos issued by my enemies, he recognized me. They have fastened me down, hunted me like an animal, and know where I am now. I know they are leaving me for the time being, because perhaps there is a bigger job – someone more important before they concentrate on the small fish. This Jew wasn't like the others. He was tall, young and blond. He was browned by the sun, he was handsome, as if he'd been in Spain as much as I had, and one day he came to the door of my garage and looked in at me. He looked, to make sure. I could not compete his stare, and they could have used my face for the chalk of Dover. How did I know he was a Jew, you ask? Don't mock me, England, because I am no longer against them. I hardly look at his face, but I *knew* because his eyes were like sulphur, a nice young man who could have been a pleasant tourist, but I knew, I knew without knowing why I knew, that he was one of their people. They have their own country now: if only they had their own country before the war, England. His eyes burned my heart away. I could not move. The next day he went off, but at any time they will come for me. I am still young, even while sixty, yet think that perhaps I don't care, that I will let them carry me, or that I will kill myself before they come.

'It is not possible I stay here, because the people have turned. Maybe the Jew told something before he went away, but a man stopped me in one of the alley-streets and said: "Guzman, get out, go home." The man had been one of my friends, so you can imagine how it bit deep at me. And then, to hammer it harder, I have been seeing it written on walls in big letters: "Guzman, go home," – which makes my brains burst, because this *is* my home. No one understands, that I am wanting to be solitary, to have peace, to labour all right. When I make tears like this I feel I am an old man.

'I should not have killed those people. I sat down to eat. They were hungry in the snow, and I could not stop myself. I could not tolerate the way they stood and looked, people who couldn't work because they had no food to take into them. They kept looking, England, they kept looking. I thought: their life is agony. I will end it. If I feed them Christmas food for three months they will never be strong again. I wanted to help them out of their life and suffering, to get them peace, so that they would be no more cold and hungry. I fired my gun. My way went terrible after that, out of control. I was rational. My soul was black. I killed and killed, to stop the spread of the suffering that came on to me. While I killed I was warm, and not aware of the suffering, the rheumatism of my soul. How could I have done it? I wasn't like the others. I was an artist.

'Look, don't go yet. Don't stand and leave me by. The sun is making that mountain drink fire. I shall always see mountains on fire, whenever I go and wherever else my feet tread, red mountains shaking flames out of their hat top. Even before the Jew came a dream was in me one night. I was a young scholar at the highschool, and circles were painted in the concrete groundspaces, for gymnasium games and drill. I stood in one, with a book in my hand to read. Everything changed, and the perfect circle was of white steel. A thin rod it was, a hot circle that glowed metal. I wanted to get out of it but I couldn't, because the heat from it was scorching my ankles. All the force of me was pressing against it, and though I was a highgrown man I couldn't jump out. I had a gun in my hand instead of a book, and I was going to shoot myself, because I knew the idea that if I did I should get out and be able to walk off a freed man. I shot someone passing by, a silent bullet. But then I woke, and nothing had worked for me.

'In military life they say there is a marshal's rank in every soldier's kitbag. In peace-life I think there is a pair of worn sandals in every cupboard, because you don't ever know when the longest life-trudge is going to start – whether you are criminal or not. I dig blame into my heart like donkey-dung into good soil. If I was an aristocrat I could claim that all my uncles had been hung up on meat-hooks because they tried to revolt. If I was from a factory I could say I didn't know any better. Everybody who dies dies in vain, England, so I can't do that. What shall I do? Your questions are pertinent, but I am practical. I am rational. I won't give in, because I am always rational. Maybe it is the best thing of quality obtained from my father. I look at my maps, and have the big hope of a hunted man. Do you have any dollars in currency that I could exchange? You haven't? Can you pay the repair bill on your car in dollars, then? Ah, so. I have another Volkswagen I could sell you, only a year old and going like a spark, guaranteed for years on rough roads. The man I bought it from had taken it to Nyasaland – overearth, the whole return. Pay me in pound-sterling then, in Gibraltar if you like. I can get the ferry there and back in a day, make my purchasing of necessaries for a long trek ... no, you can't?

'It is going to be a cloudy day, good for driving because it will be not too hot. Your car is now in excellent order, and will run well for long hours. It is a reasonable car, with a stout motor and strong frame. It it not too logical for repairing, and will not have such long life as you thought when you bought it. Next time, if you want some of my best caution, you will purchase a Volkswagen. You won't regret it, and will always remember me for giving you such solid advice.

'I am tired after being up all night. Mind how you drive, on those mountain curves. Don't you see what it speaks in the sky over there? You don't? Your eyes are not good. Or perhaps you are deceiving me to save my feelings. It says: GUZMAN, GO HOME. Where can I go? I own two houses and my garage here. I own property, England, property. All my life I have wanted to own property, and shall have to sell it to them in Villa Oveja for next door to nothing. Go home, they say to me, go home.

'Rational and intelligent! Everybody is being rational and intelligent. What beautiful words – but they have to be kept in a case and admired, like those two parrots that the hotel keeper brought back from a trip to South America. You look at them, and their beauty gives you heart. An unfortunate American client once wanted to touch them, put his finger too close to the bars, and then the blood flowed after the razor-beak snapped over it. Their colour gives you soul also, but when you are at last hunted down, and only the corner wall is behind you, then what use are being rational and intelligent? Use them, and slowly rolls the big destruction. Hitler made them kill each other in every man jackboot of us.

'I am light-headed when I don't sleep the dark, but I must go to work, think some more while I am working. My name is not Guzman. That is a name the Spaniards gave me, proud, sly, and envious, because of my clever business ways. It has always surprised me that I could make my commerical career so well, when I started off life only as a poor hiker drawing faces. Now I am a wanderer, when I don't want to be.'

Chris, his face the grey-green colour of a living tree branch that had had the bark stripped from it, turned away and walked quickly through the quiet town to the hotel. His wife was feeding the baby. The day after tomorrow, they would be in Africa. Six months after that, back in London.

The car broke down again in Tangier. 'That crazy Nazi,' he thought, 'can't even mend a bloody car.'